STARLIGHT

LISA HENRY

To all the readers who wanted more of Brady's story.

Starlight

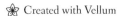 Created with Vellum

ACKNOWLEDGMENTS

Thank you to my awesome beta readers, Sofia, Katey, and Infinite World, for all your help.

And a huge thank you to Sylvia and Kat, ~~who bullied me until it was done~~ kept me motivated the entire way through!

CONTENTS

CHAPTER 1

Some days gliding through the black was quiet and peaceful like night swimming, when the universe felt like warm water lapping around my skin and left the remembered taste of salt on my lips. Some days turning my face towards the nearest star felt almost the same as turning it towards sunlight, eyes closed and toes digging in red dirt, my body warm and my heartbeat steady.

Then, other days, shit just exploded in my face with barely any warning at all.

The sudden low hiss of escaping pressure sounded like the voice of a Faceless, and then Cam was yelling:

"Brady! Get down!"

I hit the floor and the blast felt like it shattered my eardrums. A wave of heat washed over me, like a heavy blanket thrown over my back and then pulled instantly away. The air tasted like scorched metal, like burning, like Kopa. It was enough that for a second I didn't know where I was. I couldn't hear anything except a high-pitched whine vibrating in my skull. I was unanchored, caught in that place between asleep and awake, in that blank empty place that's filled with nothing—no time, no place, no *self*— right before awareness came slipping back in. Then Cam was crouching over me, hands running over me as he checked for damage, bringing me back.

The med bay. We were in Doc's med bay on the Faceless ship, and I was lying face-down on the floor, Cam's hand on the back of my neck, squeezing just tight enough to keep me anchored there.

"Are you okay?"

I rolled onto my back and blinked up at him. "What the fuck just happened?"

"The tank blew," he said, helping me to my shaky feet.

"Fuck." I stared around the room, my heart doing its level best to force its way out of my ribcage.

Andre and Doc were staring back at me. Andre was as big-eyed as an owl. He was still hugging the second tank to his chest. At least it hadn't been that one that had blown.

The oxygen tanks had been part of our supplies when we'd come aboard the Faceless ship. But the seals had degraded quickly in the humidity of the ship, and then yesterday it had been hot. Hotter than usual. The light inside the ship had taken on a strange reddish tint as we'd swept close to something that might have been a supernova. Might have been fucking anything, for all I could tell.

And *close* was relative, but what were a few million miles out in the endless black?

"You okay?" Cam asked me again.

"Yeah," I said, huffing out a breath and shaking my arms out to get the blood back into my fingers. "But I'm not fucking going near the tanks again."

It had been a close call, probably. Of the two tanks stored in Doc's makeshift med bay, Andre had already taken one from the rack and was almost at the door when I'd reached for the second one. We'd been trying to dispose of them safely by walking them to an airlock. Turned out we were a little late.

Andre carried his tank very slowly away, holding it as gingerly as though it was a newborn.

"Hell," Doc said mildly.

I followed his gaze.

A ragged piece of metal from the tank was sticking out of the damp, porous wall. As we watched, it was slowly sucked into the wall, like the ship was devouring it.

Walls. Rooms. Windows. Jesus, we didn't even have words for what those things were on the Faceless ship. Our words brought to mind right angles and hard edges, spaces measured out in cubic meters, but that's not what they were. Nothing here spoke of manufacture as much as it did of life, or maybe of mutation. The walls of the Faceless ship pulsed. Things moved behind the membranes of the walls like platelets in a bloodstream and bloomed from the walls like algae. Sometimes noises thrummed through the humid air and it sounded almost like whale songs. The ship wasn't a machine. I didn't know what the fuck it was, but it wasn't a machine.

I heard hissing again. In my skull this time. The sound of it ended on an upward note just like a question. I think they'd learned that intonation from us.

Cam rubbed his thumb over my cheekbone. "We're okay," he told the ship, told the others, told the Faceless. "We're all okay."

The Faceless had weakened the psychic connection we shared, but not severed it. We could still understand them when they spoke, but we were no longer overwhelmed by hearing every fucking random thought that slid into each other's skulls. There was an echo, though. Blowback, or something. If I cleared my mind, I could sense Andre nearby. I could sense Chris and Harry. I could hear the faint whisper of their distant conversation, and Harry's relieved laugh. A bright echo of it washed up against me, even though their words were indistinct in my mind. Cam was closer. His touch still anchored me. I could feel his concern bleeding into me, layered through with a hundred different emotions: the residual sharp edge of fear left over from the blast, his competing relief, his protectiveness, his love.

The connection wasn't as invasive as it had been back when I'd had half of fucking intel living in my head, or even back when it had just been me and Cam. It was only the faintest echo of the original that the Faceless had been unable to excise, because without it we wouldn't be able to communicate with them at all.

"How many tanks have we got left in storage?" I asked.

"Eight."

"Fuck."

"Yeah." Cam sighed. "We'll suit up to do the rest."

I knew he didn't mean atmo suits. He meant Faceless body armor, that strange liquid film that molded itself to the wearer. It was impenetrable as far as we could tell. In the generations we'd been at war with the Faceless—a strange word for what amounted to the Faceless swatting us like insects whenever they found our buzzing annoying—the military had sure as shit found nothing that could breach it, anyway. Like everything to do with the Faceless it remained a fucking mystery.

We'd been with them for three months now, as best as we could tell, and we still knew next to nothing about them.

"Give us a few minutes," Cam said to Doc, and drew me outside into the hallway where we were alone as we could be in this place where the walls between us were so porous, where we could still experience each other's emotions. "You okay?" he asked me again, curling his fingers through mine.

"Yeah." I shrugged. Grinned. "Scheduled daily freak out, you know."

"Yeah." Cam leaned in close. He knew it wasn't really a joke. Cam always knew. "That was a close call though."

"I think..." I closed my eyes. "I think that maybe I don't have the right sort of brain for this."

When I opened my eyes again he was smiling and shaking his head.

"I mean, you guys all look at the black and you're fucking fearless, you know? You're just itching to see more, to learn more. And I just think about all the shit out here that could kill us."

His smile faded. "I think of that stuff too, Brady. It's just, on balance, I think it's worth it."

"Yeah. I get that. I just can't make myself believe it, you know?"

"I know," Cam said.

I squeezed his hand tighter. "Sorry."

"Don't be sorry." The corner of his mouth quirked. "Brady Garrett doesn't apologize."

That pulled a smile out of me. "You're right."

He laughed and kissed me.

So maybe it wasn't so bad. Maybe this fear I had inside me had nothing to do with the Faceless or with the big black. Maybe, back on Earth, I'd be just as scared of not knowing what was coming next. Because nobody knew that. I learned from the time I was a kid that there were no certainties in life and no solid ground under my feet. I'd been scared of falling ever since, of losing the few people I had.

But also, this one time I made a deal with myself that I was done with being scared. I was still working on that, I guessed, and maybe I always would be, but it could only cripple me if I let it. And I wasn't going to let that happen.

Neither was Cam.

Cam circled his arms around me, and hooked his fingers through my belt loops. "Whatever happens, Brady, we've got this. We've got each other. And that's more than a lot of people get."

"Yeah." I squeezed my eyes shut for a moment and leaned back into his warmth. Borrowed a little of it, like always. "I know it is. I know."

He brushed his lips against the hinge of my jaw.

I kept my eyes closed.

From somewhere nearby, I heard Lucy shriek with laughter. The sound receded as she raced away with Harry chasing after her. Lucy's sudden happiness burst as bright as sunlight against me. For a fraction of a second it lit up my whole universe and it left me smiling.

I felt the curve of Cam's lips against my jaw as he smiled too.

He kept holding me though, and I didn't tell him to stop.

Cam splayed his fingers over my chest, over my fast-thumping heart. "I'll get Chris and Harry to help with the other tanks if you want a break."

Sometimes it was still hard for me to read his expression. Or to at least not read his concern for me as pity, like I was just a weak kid totally out of my fucking depth. Because I struggled with that shit every damn day. It was bad enough when it came from the voice in my head. I didn't need it coming from Cam as well. It was hard, sometimes, not to throw it straight back in his face like it was an insult. But I was learning.

"Yeah." I was still shaky from the blast. "I could use a break."

He moved his hand and curled it around the back of my neck. Squeezed gently, but it was enough to fill me with warmth. "I'll come find you when we're done."

"Okay. Be careful."

"Always." He flashed me a smile, and I headed back toward our quarters.

Walking through the strange pulsing corridors of a Faceless ship like they were almost home.

Jesus.

There wasn't a day when it didn't hit me in some way.

I never had any big plans for my life. Never had any ambitions apart from survival, and what was that except the craziest fantasy of all? But somehow here I was, caught up in a story far too big for a reffo from Kopa, half a universe away from the red dirt and the taste of salt on my lips. On a Faceless ship, with starlight in our slipstream.

There were no words for the wonders of the black. The horrors. Same thing. Both so massive in scale, so beyond our comprehension that we hadn't yet invented the language to describe the things we saw. And the words we had could only fail.

Every day—

Even a simple little word like 'day' lost all point of reference in space, in that weird place where time and speed and light become the same thing, and all mashed up together until they were meaningless.

Every day Cam and Chris and the others tried to chip away at the swirling universe with their words. Sometimes they wrote reports filled with the dry, precise language of science. Sometimes that wasn't enough and so they slipped a little into poetry. But even poetry couldn't reach the heights it needed to snatch understanding, to snag onto starlight and to hold it.

Every day Lucy drew pictures of space, sighing unhappily because the collection of pens she'd got on Defender Three didn't run to enough colors. At least she knew her limitations. Cam and Chris and the others kept knocking their heads against the wall without even knowing they were doing it.

Pushing that big rock up the hill day after day, or whatever.

It was very much an exercise in futility. Even if we got back to Earth, how could we translate the wonders? The horrors?

When I was a kid I saw a magic show on television. The guy made a rabbit disappear. It's always a rabbit, right? Always a rabbit, always a top hat, and always a too-wide smile when he shows the empty hat. Even when I was a kid and had never seen the trick before, I knew what to expect. *Tap tap tap* on the hat with his wand, some magic words, and the rabbit was gone. What I didn't expect was the sudden sick feeling I got inside my stomach when the magician showed the inside of that hat. You shouldn't get applause for revealing an empty void and making little kids stare into it.

That night I had a nightmare and woke my dad with my screaming.

I was still having nightmares, only this time I didn't always have to close my eyes.

I walked into our quarters and found myself drawn to the window, to what lay behind it. I stared past the filmy membrane of the window into the black, into the swirling void, and imagined what it would feel like if the stars suddenly began to blink out, one by one.

The seven of us shared a room. I mostly hung around there all the time, when everyone else was off learning everything they could and staring in wonder at the universe that washed past us in tendrils of bleeding color. I had to dig deeper to find the wonder. I had to get through the horror first. I was trying though. Every day I was trying.

"Brady?"

I turned around.

Harry was standing in the doorway, Lucy hanging off his back like a long-legged monkey.

"Yeah?"

"You okay?"

"Why wouldn't I be?"

Harry just raised his eyebrows.

Right. The explosion.

"I'm good," I told Harry. "Just, whatever."

Lucy slid off his back. "You're looking at the stars. You don't *like* the stars."

"I like the stars," I told her, slinging an arm around her when she got close, and pulling her even closer. "It's the millions of miles of black between them that fucking scares me."

"Swear jar," Lucy said, and held out her cupped hand.

Who the fuck told her about swear jars anyway? She sure as shit didn't learn it from me.

"Your hand is not a jar," I told her. We didn't have a jar, but that wasn't stopping her.

She shoved her hand in my face. "Close enough."

Lucy was my little sister. She was eight years old, and smarter than I'd been at that age. Smarter than I was now, probably.

I felt in my pockets for something to give her and found a left-over cracker from breakfast that only had a bit of fluff stuck to it. Lucy beamed as I dropped it in her palm. Three months—more or less, but who could count the days out here?—on a Faceless ship and she thought a cracker was a prize.

Still, Lucy had adapted better than I had. She didn't complain when we ran out of chocolate and she was one of the first to try the food the Faceless ate. Or not ate, exactly. They didn't eat. When they were tired or hurt or hungry they stepped into the little alcoves hidden all around the ship, and the ship rested them and healed them and fed them. They were like ticks burrowing into the flesh of an animal, feeding on its blood. And Lucy hadn't freaked out or anything when Kai-Ren showed her the alcoves.

Just stepped right in and let the walls of the ship ooze closed around her.

And I'd just stood there and stared, and waited for the magician to show me the void where the rabbit had been.

Since then I'd screwed my courage and used the alcoves as well. It was like sinking into warm water when the walls closed, but I still preferred to eat the human way. If I didn't chew and swallow, my brain still thought I was hungry, even if my stomach didn't.

Lucy snapped the cracker in two and offered half to Harry.

He flashed a grin at me as he ate it.

Asshole.

We'd run out of supplies soon, and there'd be no more crackers, just like there was already no more chocolate. I was rationing myself to only a few cigarettes a day as well, and it was fucking killing me. I got an itch under my skin just from thinking about running out.

Everyone else had adapted better than I had. Chris and Andre and Harry had trained for this shit, as much as anyone could train for the unknown, and Cam had lived with the Faceless before, but even Doc and Lucy were doing better than me. And Lucy was fucking *eight*.

"Cam wants me to help get rid of the rest of the tanks," Harry said. "That seem like the sort of thing that could come back and bite us in the ass, to you? Jettisoning our emergency oxygen?"

I shrugged. "Better it bite us in the ass in the future than literally blow up in our faces today."

Harry winced. "Good point."

It was the only fucking point, actually. Every decision we'd made since coming aboard the ship had been about choosing what might harm us later instead of what might harm us now. Guys like Harry didn't like choices like that. Guys like Harry hadn't grown up in Kopa.

Maybe I brought something to the team after all: years of finely tuned fatalism.

"I'll catch you guys later," Harry said.

"Yeah. Try not to explode."

"That's the plan," Harry told me with a grin, and headed off.

Lucy and I sat on my bunk and played Go Fish.

Scared and bored. Bored and scared. Sometimes it felt like the military had stripped me of the ability to feel any other emotion when they'd shoved me in an itchy uniform and bad-fitting boots the day I'd turned sixteen, and blasted me into the black.

Then Lucy laughed when she won, and then I felt Cam's presence at the edge of my consciousness, safe and solid, and I knew that was nothing but bullshit.

IT TOOK the guys a while to get rid of the tanks. Lucy was sick of playing Go Fish long before that. I went with her to grab her pens from where she'd left them in Doc's makeshift medbay. I pressed my hand against the wall where the metal from the exploding tank had been sucked in. It gave a little against the pressure of my touch, and my fingers dipped inside, piercing the viscous outer layer. Inside was warm. Wet and spongy. My fingertips tingled as tiny sparks zipped around them. I withdrew my hand again. I wondered if the metal had dissolved, or if it had been carried away like a jagged acanthocyte in a bloodstream.

There was nothing here I understood.

I pushed it away whenever I could. Forced myself not to look it in the eye.

Sometimes I could almost forget where I was. Sometimes, when I was sharing a cigarette with Doc or messing around with Cam or trading insults with Chris, sometimes I almost forgot. But then I'd feel one of them at the edges of my consciousness, cold and curious. The Faceless.

Faceless, and nameless too, except for Kai-Ren.

I was heading back to our quarters when I sensed him. I turned, and saw him standing there with two others.

I knew instinctively which one he was, even though it should have been impossible. Three identical Faceless in their black, gleaming body armor, tall and silent and terrifying.

There would always be a part of me that knew them from my nightmares. That only saw the cold-blooded killing machines that had burned most our cities off the face of the planet without a twinge of anything even resembling conscience. They would always be alien, and there was nothing in the universe that could ever bridge that completely. Just because we could communicate now, just because Kai-Ren was curious enough to listen to the buzzing of the little insects called humanity didn't mean that he would ever truly understand us, or that we would ever truly understand him.

But he was my savior too.

I moved toward the Faceless, toward Kai-Ren, and exhaled slowly when he reached out and rubbed his gloved hand over my hair. My hair had grown out in the months I'd been here. It no longer crinkled and prickled under his touch. It was longer now, sticking up at weird angles. It gave Cam something to twist his fingers in when I blew him. We both liked that.

"Bray-dee." Kai-Ren said my name with a hum of pleasure.

I stepped into his space, and slid my hand down his chest.

It had felt wrong at first, doing this. Touching and being touched. It had felt like a betrayal of the same touches I shared with Cam, but it wasn't.

Not...not when he didn't understand us. He liked us. He liked our warmth, our sudden bursts of irrational emotion, our strangeness. We caught his attention. We pleased him, like shiny baubles pleased some ancient king. Sometimes it felt as though we were always teetering on the brink of greater understanding, of actual meaningful communication—Cam certainly believed Kai-Ren saw us as more than interesting little diversions—but I thought that maybe we were just too different. Just because Kai-Ren liked to get caught in the echo chamber of our emotions, of our love, our fear, our hope, didn't mean he understood them.

Where Cam saw tentative connections between us, twisting

and shining like fishing line in the water, I only ever saw dark, empty space.

Kai-Ren hissed under his breath, and the other two Faceless melted away.

"Bray-dee. Little one." He plucked at my T-shirt with his gloved fingers, pulling it free from the waistband of my pants. Even with the glove, his touch was cool. The ship was humid, but the Faceless were cold-blooded. Kai-Ren moved his hand along my abdomen and my muscles jumped under his touch. His other hand gripped my jaw lightly, and he turned my face from side to side as though he was searching it for something.

He saved me, once.

Twice.

He saved me.

He saved all of us.

Humanity still lived and breathed and crawled around on the spinning ball of dirt we called Earth because of Kai-Ren. It's not so difficult to worship the unknowable power that holds your life in its hands. It's human nature. A thousand religions were built on it. Merciful gods are only a new creation. Scratch the surface and underneath they're all fed on blood and fear.

I tried not to flinch as Kai-Ren slid his fingers past my waistband.

He hissed again, and released me.

"Kai-Ren!" Lucy rounded the bend of the corridor, clutching her pens.

"Lu-cee."

Lucy grinned, and slid her hand into his. "I drew you a picture! Do you want to see it?"

A braver man, or maybe a smarter one, would have seen this moment for what it was. Seen him for what he was. A predator. A nightmare. Should have seen the death's head under that black mask, should have seen that he was a cold-blooded thing.

But I wasn't, and I didn't, and all because of the pleased hum he made when Lucy curled her fingers through his.

I let my chattering little sister draw Kai-Ren away from me.

Just stared and let it happen, and reminded myself again that he had saved us all. The nightmare, the savior; they were the same thing, and I still hadn't reconciled that. Still hadn't found a way to stop my heart from trying to beat out of my chest when he was close. I probably never would.

Kai-Ren had never hurt her. I knew he wouldn't.

I *knew* that, or told myself I did.

But knowing was never enough to kill the fear at the heart of me. Fear was just another thing the universe let build up, let feed on itself until it was big enough to shatter me over and over again, and then send the fragments spinning into the black.

Fear was one of the few things I understood.

Without it, I would be adrift.

CHAPTER 2

ON THE FACELESS ship we debriefed every night. Doc had insisted on that from the first day, just like he'd insisted we keep to a regular schedule like the one the military had drilled into us for years. Doc had brought a clock with him from Defender Three. It was an old wind-up clock with hands instead of a digital display. Our lives were ruled by that little clock. Time was arbitrary, out here more than anywhere, but Doc made sure we had day and night, every hour counted and accounted for.

At first the Faceless thought it was strange, the way we'd stay in our room and sleep from ten until six. And it had felt strange too. There was no dimming of the lights at night on the Faceless ship like there had been on the station, and no turning them on again in the morning. But Doc's insistence of sticking to a routine had stopped us from going crazy in those first few weeks probably.

Bringing a clock that didn't need batteries had been smart. It only took about a week for all the tablets to run down. We'd started with twelve solar powered chargers but were running through them at a rate of knots. Sometimes there wasn't enough light outside the ship for them to get any juice and at least one of them had been completely ruined when we skirted too close to something that looked a lot like an electrical storm, but probably wasn't. What the fuck did I know about what was out here?

We debriefed in our room. Even Lucy joined us, lying on the top bunk above mine and drawing pictures while we went over everything we'd done that day.

"Well, we've lost our oxygen tanks," Doc growled, puffing on a cigarette. He was sitting on his trunk, knees apart, big hands dangling into the space between them. He had the hands of a rugby player, not a surgeon, but I'd seen him with those hands shoved up the wrists in the guts of some guy and I knew they were deceptive. "I checked the seals on the atmo suits as well, and they've all corroded. They're useless."

He dragged the toe of his boot across the damp, spongy floor.

The first week or so we were onboard we'd tried to keep our stuff dry and clean, but the air itself was damp and humid so it was impossible. The Faceless ship had been hard on our gear. We were mostly using notebooks instead of datapads, and not just because we were fast running out of ways to charge the datapads.

"Can we fix the seals?" Chris Varro asked.

"No idea," Doc said, puffing out a mouthful of smoke. "It's possible we can use some of the Faceless goo in a pinch, but I wouldn't want to gamble my life on it. Or anyone's."

Chris nodded, his brow furrowed, pacing back and forth in front of the strange filmy window. Stars slid slowly past behind him and I tore my gaze away.

"Fried another solar charger today," Andre said from his bunk.

Chris stopped pacing. "Another one?"

Andre nodded. "We're down to six now."

"Shit," Chris said.

"Swear jar!" Lucy announced from the bunk above mine, her skinny legs and bare feet swinging in my field of vision.

The humidity on the Faceless ship was probably going to wreck our canvas bunks too—even on those rare days it was inexplicably cold everything was still so fucking wet—but Lucy was light enough that she wouldn't hurt too much if she crashed on top of me one night. Chris was probably the one who had most to worry about on that account: Andre was built like a tank.

Harry, leaning on the wall with his arms crossed over his chest, laughed when Chris hunted through his pockets for something to appease Lucy with. He came up with a sachet of sugar he must have saved from a ration pack, and tossed it up towards Lucy.

I didn't like Chris much, and I hadn't since the day I'd met him on Defender Three after I'd shared all Cam's memories of fucking and being fucked by the guy. Of *loving* him. I'd felt for him the things Cam had felt when they'd been together, and the asshole had looked right through me.

It hadn't been his fault, but it had stung.

There was also the time that his buddies in intel had beaten the crap out of me, and the time they'd put Cam and me in a cell underground. Neither of those things had been Chris's ideas, but he hadn't exactly objected too hard either. Chris had come through for me since, but we were never going to be friends. Chris was better looking than me, and smarter than me, and he'd had Cam first.

Cam, sitting beside me on my bunk, caught my eye like he'd sensed my mood souring. Maybe he had. Maybe everyone had. Maybe my jealousy washed through the whole ship like the last dregs of moonshine you swirled in the bottom of the bottle while you braced yourself to swallow it down, and then it burned the whole way.

"Yeah." Andre shrugged his massive shoulders. "We need to figure out some way to charge our equipment using the ship's power. But everything here is..."

I glanced at the wall as a cluster of bioluminescent platelets burbled through it. Power thrummed all around us, but how the fuck were we supposed to plug anything in?

"It's a moot point anyway," Cam said, "since everything corrodes so rapidly. The datapads won't last much longer than the chargers."

"Okay." Chris nodded, worry tugging the edges of his mouth

down. He dipped his head, and it threw the dark shadows under his eyes into stark relief. For a moment his face looked like a skull, the eye sockets empty. A death's head, or maybe a Faceless. And then he looked up again, and the illusion vanished and he just looked tired.

Despite Doc's insistence on maintaining a routine, Chris didn't sleep much. It was like he was working on a deadline only he could feel. Like he couldn't get more than a few hours sleep at a time before he was driven from his bunk with the urge to work. I didn't even know what the hell he did every day, except he knew the Faceless ship better than the rest of us. He was always checking something new out and coming back to the room with pages and pages of notes.

"So we just make the move completely to paper and pencils," Chris said. "And hope we don't run out."

"We still don't know anything about how Faceless tech works," Harry said. "If we could find a way to make it compatible with ours, we could use it, and then transfer all the data back whenever we get back to a Defender."

"Faceless tech is synapses and blood and brain chemistry," Doc said. "We're already using Faceless tech—it's how we can talk to them. They plugged us in to it via an infection. Well..." He snorted. "Well, Rushton was plugged in by the Faceless. The rest of us did it to ourselves. Still, it's biological, not mechanical. It's technology, but I don't think it's the sort we can upload files on, anymore than we can upload them to another person's brain."

Just another word we had to rewrite the definition for when it came to the Faceless then. Just another concept we barely had the language to explain.

"That's not exactly true though," Chris said. He rolled his shoulders like he was trying to release the tension he was holding in them. "There's this thing near the base of the helix that spins like a turbine. That has to be manufactured. I can't believe biology can be that precise."

Doc huffed, and sucked in a lungful of smoke. "They're *aliens*, Varro. Whole fucking universe right outside that window, and you think biology's bound by what you know about from Earth? Those rules don't apply out here in the black. And for all we know somewhere out there is a species that shits perfect equilateral triangles!"

"Swear jar!" Lucy exclaimed, and Doc grumbled as he went through his pockets.

Doc had a point though.

This wasn't a scientific mission, and we sure as shit weren't scientists. Chris and Andre and Harry were from intel, but there were no codes to crack here, no information to sift through looking for patterns. The Faceless were too different than us. Our frames of reference were useless here, as useless as our datapads and oxygen tanks and atmo suits.

And if the guys from intel were useless, the rest of us were even worse. Cam and Doc and Lucy and me were just the extras. At least Doc could contribute on the research side of things, and Cam was smart enough to keep up with the others, but Lucy and I weren't exactly pulling our weight. If we ever made it back to Earth, nobody would be publishing any research papers by Brady or Lucy Garrett. We were just a pair of reffos along for the ride.

We drew pictures and we told stories about what we remembered from Kopa and our dad, and every day I saw the echo of him in Lucy's smile and heard him in her laugh.

Sometimes I wondered what my dad would say if he could see us now. His kids, drifting in the stars. I liked to think he would have smiled at that, and said something about how he always knew we were made for more than Kopa. That was probably just a fantasy though. How could he even have imagined something like that? My dad's world had been a small one, a narrow one. Men like him didn't get to dream.

I figured that maybe me and Lucy could do the dreaming for him.

I didn't know.

We were both alive, and that was miraculous.

We were also on a Faceless ship, and most days I couldn't tell the difference between the miracle and the nightmare.

Just fucking semantics maybe, but it prickled at my consciousness all the time, like some sort of scab I couldn't leave alone. How could I come to terms with something I couldn't even define? How could I process a thing I couldn't even fucking articulate?

It left me with nothing but nausea. It was the sort of nausea that had more to do with Doc's philosophy books than his medical ones, I think. I probably shouldn't have read them at all, but what else was there to do?

The hours and days all bled together on the Faceless ship just like they had on Defender Three, really. Mostly I did what I'd done there. I kept my head down and tried to avoid work. Back on Defender Three I'd been counting down the days until the military let me go home again. It didn't work like that here. How could it? Time wasn't just arbitrary out here—it was meaningless.

I didn't have the same anger in me here though; the same low flare that burned in my gut and itched at the base of my skull, day in and day out, until I was wired enough to lash out and get in a fight just to break the fucking tension. Here, Lucy was with me. I was looking after her, just like our dad had wanted. I had Cam as well, and he was more than I'd ever dared to hope for.

Cam saw better things in me than I ever saw in myself.

He caught me looking at him, and leaned in closer. He reached around behind me and hooked a finger through the belt loop of my pants, like he just wanted to keep me close and remind me that I was his. I liked it.

"The Faceless have weapons that blasted our cities off the face of the planet," Chris said, unwilling to let shit go, just like always. He got an idea fixed in his head and he went with it. And he might not have been a scientist, but he had that same need to assign everything a classification. To create order out of chaos by putting labels on things. "You really think that's biological tech?"

Doc stubbed his cigarette out on the top of the footlocker. "Why the hell not? You ever heard of a bombardier beetle? Irreducible complexity is a fallacy. If evolution can give us a beetle that shoots boiling acid out of its ass, why not some sort of weapon that could destroy a city? We've been on this ship for months now, and I've yet to see anything that looks like it came from a factory or a store. The Faceless aren't monkeys with tools like us, Varro. They're insects in a hive."

Command should have sent a team of entomologists instead of a bunch of guys from intel, probably.

I could tell Chris didn't like Doc's answer though, and not just from the frustration that rolled out of him in waves and crashed up against the rest of us. It was written all over his face. His brow furrowed again and his mouth turned down. From what I'd seen of Chris in our shared memoires—from what I'd *felt* of him—he was the kind of guy who didn't like puzzles he couldn't solve, and there was no bigger puzzle in the universe than the Faceless. Chris had figured his out-of-the-box thinking when it came to this mission might be the thing that cracked it once and for all. The idea that Doc might be right and the Faceless could remain entirely incomprehensible to us was one that sat like a rock in his gut. Chris wanted to be the guy who saved the entire planet from the Faceless by coming up with a way we could actually negotiate with them, but how could we?

It was impossible.

Kai-Ren liked us. We amused and interested him. And once, accidentally, my anger and fear and heartbreak had hit just the right pitch to catch his attention.

"Doc's right. They're like insects," I said. I withdrew my crumpled cigarette packet from my pocket, and lit one. "They're not individuals, not the way we are. Can you even imagine how crazy we seem to them? Over a billion people, all with our own thoughts and ambitions, crammed onto one tiny little planet. It must look like a fucking mess to them."

There had been more than seven billion of us once, back before the Faceless left craters where our largest cities had once stood. Back before those people crawling on the surface of our tiny, fragile planet had even known to look up at the stars in terror instead of wonder. They never even saw it coming.

Sometimes I envied them for that.

It was our chaos that fascinated Kai-Ren though. That individuality. Cam had been a stoic captive. Not me. I'd kicked and screamed and rattled the cage with my panic.

A spark of remembered fear shivered through me, and I ducked my head to avoid Chris's gaze.

Cam brushed his fingers over my thigh, just a light touch to remind me he was there.

"There's always common ground," Chris said at last, like speaking the words with conviction would somehow make them true. "Something to build on. There has to be."

I shrugged, and didn't bother answer him. What was there to say? If Chris wanted to keep pushing that rock up the hill, day in and day out, who the fuck was I to tell him to quit?

He'd figure it out in the end, or die trying.

Doc cleared his throat and we moved on to talking about rations and what we were going to run out of next, not that there was anything we could do about it anyway.

All our debriefings were exercises in fatalism, one way or another.

BACK HOME IN KOPA, by the creek, there had been a bunch of massive Moreton Bay fig trees, or banyans. Each tree grew outward, dropping roots down from their branches in tendrils, their insides hollowing out as they expanded. Some of the old people used to tell stories handed down to them about how before Kopa had been a township—before it had been much of anything at all—when cyclones swept in from the sea the people used to shelter inside the banyans, hidden in the hollows, crouching there as the storm outside raged. We used to play in those empty spaces when I was a kid. It was dark and cool inside, with spots of dappled sunlight on the dirt floor where the light filtered through the twisted mesh of the buttress roots.

Parts of the Faceless ship were like that. Roots and tendrils and empty spaces. The bones of the ship were dark though, and smooth, not at all like the rough surface of the banyan trees. But even in the darkest places on the Faceless ship there was faint light. Weird greenish light, like bioluminescence. It was in the bloodstream of the ship itself, in the weird floating platelets that pulsed through the walls and the strange skeleture of the ship.

There was a damp little recess in a wall a few decks up from our room, and I went and sat there after the evening debriefing. Not that there were actual decks on a Faceless ship, with stairs or elevators or anything. Instead, everything was built on a spiral. A helix, Chris called it, like the inside of the shells I sometimes used to find on the beach back at Kopa: one continuous curving thread that twisted slowly upward. There was nothing special about this recess. It was just a place where Cam and I met up, far enough away from the others that they wouldn't stumble over us unless they were looking, and away from the areas the Faceless seemed to frequent the most. It was about the same size as the alcoves the ones the Faceless slept in and ate in, but it didn't seem to do anything. We'd pressed on the walls when we were first scoping the place out, but they didn't open up and suck us in.

I sat on the damp floor while I waited, and closed my eyes and tried to imagine that I was in Kopa. I tried to remember how it felt to have the sunlight beating on my back and the red dirt burning the soles of my feet. Some guys were made to chase starlight in the black, but some of them, like me, were smaller than that, curled up tight like a dried, withered leaf. Brittle, with all the edges tattered and torn. Some of us weren't built to withstand the storm.

"Hey." Cam's hand was warm on the back of my neck, his thumb rubbing against the soft hair at my nape that had grown from prickles into wisps during our time onboard the Faceless ship.

"Hey."

Cam sat down beside me, his shoulder knocking against mine. He stretched his legs out. Their reach was a little longer than mine, but that was Cam all over, wasn't it? Smart, good-looking, tall. The perfect poster boy for the war effort, his handsome smile reminding us that humanity was good, that humanity was worth fighting for, or breaking your back in a factory for, or dying choking on a lungful of disease.

It wasn't Cam's fault though. Nobody had ever asked him if he wanted his face plastered all over the world.

Join the Military and Save the Earth.

Cam's face was the most famous on the planet, probably, and it rankled me more than it did him. I was never any good at sharing, and back planetside there wasn't a single fucking day that had passed when we didn't get the look: *It's Cameron Rushton! But what's he doing with that reffo?*

I was taken by the Faceless too, but nobody ever put me on a poster or in front of the media. Guess they were just too damn worried about what I might say if I opened my mouth.

"Chris is a fucking dick," I said now, picking at a hangnail.

Cam threw me a look like he was trying to figure out if I was looking for a fight or not. Hell if I knew either, honestly.

"He's not a dick," he said at last. He raised his eyebrows. "And I didn't come and find you so we could talk about Chris."

"Yeah? What'd you come and find me for then, LT?"

He leaned in closer so that his breath was hot against my cheek when he spoke. "I came to tell you I've been thinking about your dick for hours, Crewman Garrett. Thinking about how good it would feel if you fucked me."

"Is that so?" I asked, chewing on my lower lip in that way that never failed to draw his gaze. "Sounds a lot like you're advocating for some fraternization, *sir*. We could get in a lot of trouble for that."

"Well." Cam leaned away again, a smirk tugging at the corners of his mouth. "Of course I'd never ask you to break the rules, crewman."

"So you were just thinking about my dick hypothetically, sir?"

"Of course, crewman," Cam said. "Hypothetically."

Sometimes we teased each other with this dumb game for ages, but today I was already wound up and jittery and I didn't have the patience for it. I laughed, and then Cam did too, and I reached out and hauled him over so that he was straddling my lap.

He'd ditched his tunic somewhere on the way here, so he was just wearing his thin T-shirt. The damp fabric was stuck to the planes of his torso and I peeled it up so that I could run my fingers across his abdomen and watch the way the muscles moved and jerked under my touch. When Cam sucked a breath in, I slid my hand down into his pants and felt him shiver against me as I closed my hand around his cock.

The Faceless technology—nanos, a virus, what-the-fuck-ever, had left an echo in us, a kind of a feedback loop. It was strongest when we fucked. I was touching Cam, but also feeling what he did as he was touched. Wasn't just his cock I was stroking.

So we had Kai-Ren to thank for that too, I guess.

"What are you smiling about?" Cam asked, grinding into my hand, his breath hot against my mouth.

"You know," I said, rubbing my thumb over the head of his cock to make us both squirm. "The usual. I'm never entirely sure I'm alone in my own head, but at least the sex is amazing."

"Mmm." Cam caught my bottom lip between his teeth and tugged gently. Then he released me, and licked the small hurt away. "Look at you. Brady Garrett, the optimist."

"Lies." I left his cock alone for a moment to tackle his fly, and mine. He leaned up to let me shove his pants and underwear down. "I'm not an optimist. Life is bleak and the universe is meaningless and we're all gonna die."

A joke.

Just a joke, but Cam stilled. He reached out and held my face between his hands, and his gaze searched mine.

"Life is a gift," he said softly. "And the universe is a miracle, and we have each other as long as we live. And…" He brushed his lips against mine in a kiss that was way too soft for a quick fuck in a dark corner. "And I love you."

There was no echo of a lie in his heartbeat, no twist of one in his gut when he said those words. There never had been.

"Sometimes you look at me like I'm drowning, Cam," I said, swallowing around the sudden ache in my throat. "And you gotta jump in and save me a hundred times a day. Do you ever get tired of that?"

His gaze was open. His heart was too. "Never."

"I love you too," I whispered back to him, and we kissed again. Heat built between us again, slowly at first, but then faster and faster, each touch, each kiss more frantic and hungry than the last, until Cam was grinding against me and I was desperate to come, my cock throbbing and my balls aching. I was half-afraid I would before I even got inside him.

"Come on," he said, leaning down and dragging a hand along the wall, leaving his skin gleaming with shining, viscous fluid. Then he slathered it along my dick.

It was gross, if I let myself think about it, so I refused to let myself think about it. Denial was an old friend of mine. Besides, we were getting nutrients from the goo inside the walls every time we used an alcove to eat. What difference did using it for this make?

I scooped some onto my fingers, and then felt down the crease of Cam's ass to get him ready. There was a part of me that could never quite believe this. Could never quite believe that Cam was mine like this.

"Love you," I said again, just to hear his response.

"I love you too," he said, his eyes closing as my fingers breached him. "I'm ready, Brady. So ready."

He was so beautiful, and so fundamentally good, and maybe I was learning to be something of an optimist after all, because a universe where Cam was mine? Maybe this was the best of all possible universes after all.

"Fuck, *Brady*." Cam's voice was strained as I drove up into him. I loved how he let me do this. Loved how he let me take him apart. Loved how tight his ass was around my cock, and how I could feel the way tremors raced through him under my hands. Together, we made electricity.

Should have fucking harnessed that to try to get our tablets charged.

My rhythm faltered, and I smothered a laugh into Cam's throat.

"What?" he asked, his fingers digging into my shoulders.

"Sorry. Just thinking stupid stuff."

"Then fucking *focus*, Crewman Garrett."

I huffed out another laugh, "Are you seriously trying to pull rank on me when my dick's in your ass?"

"Brady!" he whined.

"I got you," I told him. "I got you, Cam." We both shuddered through the sensation as he clenched around my cock. "Fuck, yeah."

I squeezed my eyes shut, and held my breath, and tried not to come too soon.

Outside the universe was a whirling maelstrom, chaotic and beyond comprehension, but here in this dark little corner of the Faceless ship it was just us. Just Cam and me, and the electricity between us, and the faint echo of other consciousnesses touching ours like tiny waves on a distant shore, and I loved him, and I was warm for now, and safe for now, and he loved me back. This was more than I ever thought I'd get, and I was allowed this. This miracle.

"Brady. Jesus, Brady." Cam's eyes were closed, and his voice was barely louder than a breath. He threaded our fingers together and curled them around his dick. We stroked him off together, his pleasure reverberating through me, building tighter in both of us, climbing higher and higher until we were both shaking with it, our breath punched out of us every time Cam sank back down onto my cock, every time he clenched around me.

"Brady!" He came with a gasp, threads of cum dripping down our fingers, our stomachs, and I followed fast behind, pushing into him urgently like my body was afraid I'd never be allowed in him again.

Cam sprawled over me, pressing his mouth against my clavicle, breath hot and fast. I traced my fingers down his back, drawing patterns against his damp flesh. We lay there, skin to skin, catching our breath slowly as we fell through the stars.

CHAPTER 3

I WALKED with Cam back to our quarters later that night, both of us lazy and tired, but there was an itch in my skull that wouldn't let me settle. I checked that Lucy was in bed, snuffling away in the canvas bunk above mine, and then headed back outside and along the corridor, following a series of pulsing lights in the membranous walls of the ship. Doc had set up his medbay down the corridor from our shared quarters. He called it a medbay, but it was basically just a smallish room where he could sit down on his camp stool and put his feet up and read his books without the rest of us bothering him. He was sorting through his books when I found him, stacking them in his footlocker carefully so they didn't come in contact with the sticky floor.

There was a fried solar charger sitting on the floor next to his camp stool. I picked it up and turned it over in my hands. "Should've given us an engineer. Or a mechanic or a sparkie instead of a bunch of useless fucking officers."

Doc grinned at me from around the chewed pen jammed in his mouth. He was rationing cigarettes too. "Not sure there was a lot of forward planning involved in this clusterfuck of a mission, son."

I snorted at that. "You're one to talk."

Doc waggled his bushy eyebrows.

I scowled at him to hide the sudden rush of warm affection that swelled in me. Doc was here because of me. Because he knew I was scared, and he'd always looked out for me. Even when I was nothing more than a mouthy fucking recruit, he'd looked out for me. Taken me under his cranky old wing and smoothed out some of the rougher edges of my attitude problem, or at least taught me to pick my battles. Mostly. I was still kind of unteachable in that regard.

He hauled a textbook out of the stack he kept in his footlocker. "Here."

I took it. "*General Physiology*? Why the fuck would I want to read this?"

"Because if you keep reading Camus, you'll slit your fucking wrists on me," Doc said. "And because I'm promoting you to surgical assistant."

I narrowed my eyes at him. "That's a hell of a step up from mop jockey."

Doc grunted. "Well, the pay's shit."

"Seriously though, Doc, what's the point? Something goes wrong and the Faceless throw us in the pod and we're good." I smiled to drown the frisson of fear that skittered down my spine at the memory.

Twice.

That had happened to me twice. The first time I'd been beaten into a broken, bloody pulp. The second time had been asphyxiation. I wasn't going for a third time.

"Because who the hell knows how those things work?" Doc asked. "And who's to say they won't break down?"

"Fair enough." I hugged the textbook to my chest.

He grunted again.

The stuff he'd said about me and Camus wasn't that much of an exaggeration. I think we both knew the real reason he'd given me the book was to give me something to do, to stop me from climbing the walls or from having a fucking meltdown whenever I remembered exactly where I was.

"Any chance you've got a textbook on psychological disorders in there as well?" I asked, nodding at his footlocker.

"Son," Doc said, "you *are* that fucking textbook."

Fair point.

"So are you gonna give me tests on this shit?" I asked.

"Yep." Doc chewed on his pen a little more aggressively, and drew his bushy eyebrows together tightly. "Are you gonna give me attitude about it?"

"Hell yes."

He huffed out a laugh. "I don't know why I expected anything different."

"Me neither."

We gave one another shit, Doc and me, but there was more between us than that. Much more. I loved Doc. I'd never said it aloud, but he knew. He'd seen me at my worst and he'd picked me up and put me back together. He could have looked right through me like everyone else had, but Doc wasn't that kind of man. He was here, wasn't he? There was nobody in the universe who could replace my dad, but Doc was the only man who could ever come close.

He rose to his feet, grumbling as his old knees creaked. He pulled a pack of cigarettes out of his pocket. "Want one?"

"Fuck, yes!" It was the reason I'd sought him out to begin with, and he knew it. I took one eagerly. "You got any more stashed around here anywhere?"

"Not many," Doc said ruefully. "How much of an asshole are you gonna be when you're in withdrawal?"

I lit the cigarette. "I'll be your worst nightmare."

"You already are, son." His eyes crinkled when he grinned. "Guess we're quitting together then."

I inhaled, and held the burn in my lungs for as long as I could. "Guess we are."

It was going to be hell.

DAYS BLED TOGETHER on the Faceless ship, however hard Doc tried to distinguish them with his little wind-up clock. Doc, like me, didn't actually have any specific duties to perform or reports to write, but he made us debrief every day and he kept a diary. He wrote in it and made sketches and, in his own way, tried to describe the Faceless and their ship and the universe they showed us in words that would probably always fall short. Doc seemed to have come to terms with that though. His brow didn't furrow in frustration every time he tried to get something down on paper the way that Chris's did.

He also made me read at least ten pages of *General Physiology* a day, and tested me on the content. We both knew it wouldn't go anywhere—if we ever made it home I'd be mopping floors again—but it kept us both from going stir-crazy, I guess.

"You remember when you wanted to recommend me for officer training?" I asked him one day, flicking through the pages of the textbook.

He fixed me with a stare. "I meant it. You were a good trainee medic. You'd be a good paramedic as well, and that would get you your foot in the door to becoming an actual doctor."

"I quit school when I was twelve, Doc."

"So? The military would have caught you up."

"It's a moot point now," I told him. "No fucking schools out here with the Faceless. Anyway, the military was never gonna get more than ten years out of me. Not for nothing."

I was good enough to get conscripted and sent to a Defender hanging in the black, but I wasn't a citizen. I didn't even get to vote for the government that had told me when I was sixteen that they owned the next ten years of my life. So fuck them. Fuck all of them.

I met Doc's steady gaze, and felt the warm glow of his sympathy brush up against all my old anger. I was an open book, and it made me want to hunch away defensively.

"Maybe back on Earth," I said at last, mostly to dodge Doc's concern. "If me and Cam hadn't ended up back out here. Maybe, if someone there had asked me."

Except back on Earth nobody had looked at me and thought I was a doctor and an officer in the making. They'd just put a mop in my hands and pointed me toward the nearest puddle of vomit on the hospital floor. You make reffos into officers, and who the fuck knows what might happen next? They might even want to be citizens or something, and who'd die in the factories and smelters of the refugee townships if suddenly every reffo was allowed to just get up and leave?

Doc tilted his head curiously. "What do you *want*, Brady? If money was no object, if your background wasn't, and if you could do anything you wanted, what would it be?"

I shrugged. "I've got Lucy and I've got Cam. Seems to me like I'm already way ahead of the curve, Doc."

I've got you too, and you're another thing I never deserved.

He smiled, and I wondered if he'd heard that thought or if he'd just read it in my face. "Your dreams aren't even a little bigger than that, son?"

"No," I said, but I felt a stirring of unease in my gut as I said it, like it was the wrong answer, or like there was something wrong with me since I thought it was the right answer. I shrugged, staring down at the book so I could dodge Doc's gaze. "I don't know."

And what did it matter anyhow? I still had six years left in the military, and that was provided we even made it back to Earth, and provided the military didn't decide to somehow extend my period of conscription because they were a bunch of fucking assholes who could do whatever the hell they wanted, and provided the Faceless returned us like they said they would.

Jesus. Didn't Doc know that I couldn't make dreams for the future because the present was already a miracle? I was alive, and Lucy and Cam were alive, and we were together, and we were safe for now, but nothing was certain. Nothing.

I'd had dreams once where I'd open a letter and it would be

from my dad, and he would say that he'd been misdiagnosed, and that he was okay, and that he wasn't going to die. But those weren't the sorts of dreams you built a future on. Those were the sorts of dreams that took you with them when they crumbled into pieces. I'd had dreams once too where I was just a normal guy with a normal life, never hungry, never broke. Maybe that was the kind of dream Doc was talking about, but I never did figure out how to tell those dreams apart from the crazy fantasies. They were all the same from where I was looking. Or they had been, not so long ago.

"I've got Lucy and Cam," I said again, forcing a smile. "I already told you, Doc, I'm ahead of the curve."

Don't make me look at it too close, Doc. I only just started to believe in miracles. Don't make me think I can get more than this one.

Doc had that steely look in his eye like he could spent the next hour telling me all the ways I was wrong, but he must have caught an echo of the anxiety that was gnawing at my gut because he grunted and then he let it go.

He tugged his pack of cigarettes out of his pocket, and held them out of my reach. "Finish chapter four," he said. "If you get all the answers right, you can have one."

This was an old familiar pattern, where Doc was my gruff teacher and I was the recalcitrant student he had to bribe to pay attention.

It was more than that too. It was Doc letting me off the hook, and offering me a reprieve. I liked that about Doc. When Cam saw the gulf between us, he tried to bridge it, tried to make me feel like we were standing on the same side. Doc knew better.

I hunched over the textbook, and flashed him a cheeky smile that we both knew was only surface thin. "You just wait, Doc. You're gonna owe me that whole pack by the time I'm done with this book."

He grunted, and cuffed the back of my head. "I bet I will, son. I bet I will."

THAT NIGHT I woke up with a start.

Cam made a soft noise beside me, and kept sleeping.

I sat up and swung my legs over the side of the bunk. The floor was damp and sticky against my bare feet. I didn't care. Barely noticed it anymore. I just reached under the bunk and dragged my footlocker out. Opened it and found my cigarettes.

"Bad dream?" Chris Varro asked in a low voice from the bunk on the opposite wall.

I hadn't known he was awake.

I lit my cigarette. "Hot dream," I lied.

"Was I in it?"

"Fucker."

He laughed quietly.

I'd had my fair share of wet dreams about Chris. And they weren't just when I'd shared dreams with Cam. Pretty sure I'd come up with some all on my own. And I wish I could say that was the weirdest thing about my life, but it barely made the list. And if it was weird for me to be sharing a room with my boyfriend's ex, how fucking weird was it for him to see us together? At least he didn't try to pull rank on me anymore, and I didn't try to stab him in the throat with a screwdriver. We were a work in progress, Chris and me.

Chris's bunk creaked as he rose to his feet. He walked to the doorway, and beckoned me to follow.

I did.

"Those damn bunks," he said, rolling his shoulders as he led me down the slope of the corridor towards Doc's medbay. "I don't know how you and Cam can fit in a single one."

"We make it work," I said. Cam slept in the bunk next to mine in theory, but in practice we usually ended up wedged close together in the one. I wondered if Chris was jealous. I would have burned with it if I'd had to see Cam with another guy. It was bad enough I'd seen it in his memories.

Chris regarded me silently for a moment, a sort of half smile on his lips, and I remembered—I *felt*—exactly why Cam had fallen in love with him. Chris was a good-looking guy, but more than that, he was smart and he was ambitious, but not in the way a lot of military guys were. Chris didn't give a fuck about rank or prestige or how many medals they gave him. He was driven by something outside of all that. Chris wanted to unravel all the mysteries of the universe. No wonder that Cam, chasing starlight, had fallen so easily into his orbit.

They'd been perfect together, at least for a while.

"I like you, Brady," he said. He reached forward and plucked my cigarette from between my fingers. Took a drag on it, and gave it back. "You don't like me, but I like you."

"You steal my fucking cigarettes and of course I don't like you."

His smile widened. "We both know that's not the reason why."

I shrugged, because there was no point denying it.

"You're good for him," Chris said at last. Glowing platelets slid past in the wall behind him and illuminated his face for a moment. "You're good for each other."

"I know we are," I said, trying not to bristle, because I couldn't quite read him. I couldn't tell if he was being friendly, or if he was being a condescending prick and implying Cam and I needed his fucking approval or something. Usually I thought the worst of people and usually I was right, but lately I was trying to, I don't know, be a better person or some bullshit. I at least wanted to set a better example for Lucy, so that she didn't have to look at me and then look at all these other guys and wonder why I wasn't like them. I didn't want her to like them more than me because they weren't angry and afraid all the time.

Chris stared at me for a long moment, and I wasn't sure what he was looking for. "Whole universe out here," he said at last, "just like Doc says, and you're still living in your own head."

"So what if I am? No fucking law against it."

His mouth turned up in a faint smile. "Don't forget I've been inside your skull, Brady. How do you even stand it? It's so *loud* in there."

I blew smoke in his face and ignored the way my stomach twisted.

He smiled again and shook his head. When he spoke his voice was tempered with sympathy, and that's what made me hate him the most. "Whole universe out here, Brady, right in front of your eyes, and you're still too afraid to look at it, aren't you?"

"Fuck you," I said. "I'm going back to bed."

I left the asshole standing there, wreathed in the pulsating lights of the Faceless ship.

BACK WHEN I was first in Cameron Rushton's head I saw the things that he had seen in his captivity. I felt them too. I saw the inside of the Faceless ship. I felt Kai-Ren's claws on my spine, and heard the hiss of his alien speech in my ear. I saw twin suns and, once, a strange city built of twisting towers underneath a purple sky.

Back when I first met Cameron Rushton, I was corpse-pale from living for three years on a Defender but Cameron Rushton—who should have been the dead guy—had a tan.

Some days I liked to run my fingers along his skin and remember that tan. Back home he'd had a tan too. More of one than the Faceless had given him with their twin suns on their strange planet. Sometimes, on weekends, we'd caught the train to the beach. It wasn't like the beaches in Kopa with their rusted croc traps half-sunk in water, mudflats and mangroves. This was a white-sand beach with waves that broke in crisp sparkling lines off the shore and then chased each other up onto the sand. Once I got so sunburned that my nose was flaking for days afterward, and Cam, laughing, would put cool lotion on it for me. I went red and peeled in the sun. Cam tanned, because of course he did. Handsome fucker.

When we kissed on that beach, we tasted like salt.

Now, after three months in the black, Cam was almost as pale as me. The glowing lights in the wall tinged his skin blue as they pulsed by.

We were playing poker on my bunk. I was the better player, mostly because what the hell were conscripted guys meant to do to kill time out in the black? Playing against officers was like playing against a batch of homesick sixteen-year-old recruits off the latest shitbox. They were hopeless.

Also, I cheated a lot.

Cam probably knew it, but what did it matter? Not like we were playing for cash. We weren't even playing for rations. We were just playing to pass the time. And we'd done it so often that even cheating was losing its shine. Pretty sure I could recognize all the cards by the way they were bent or creased, or by the mottled patterns of damp fingerprint marks on their backs like snakeskin.

"When the Faceless took you, how long did it take to get to their planet?"

There was a flash of something unsettled in his eyes. It wasn't quite sharp enough to call fear, but even Cam wasn't as stoic about that memory as he wanted to be. How could he be? It didn't matter that the Faceless hadn't been acting with any cruel intent. Didn't matter that they were just that cold-blooded. They'd slaughtered everyone on that shitbox like they were nothing. Guys Cam must have been talking to, joking with, moments before it happened. And then Kai-Ren had taken Cam.

The nightmare had gotten worse before it had gotten better.

Cam looked away for a moment, and when he looked back his mouth was quirked. "I don't know. I didn't have a wind-up clock. I think that my sense of time was one of the first things I lost."

Not the last thing though. Not by a long shot.

It was unthinkable to me that Cam had been able to bring himself to step foot on a Faceless ship again, but he'd always been braver than me. Smarter. Better. And the thing I loved most about him was that he never even saw it.

I felt a prickling presence at the edge of my consciousness, and turned my head to look. There was a Faceless standing in the doorway. It didn't feel familiar in the way that Kai-Ren did. It stood watching us silently. Nothing threatening about it at all, apart from its appearance. And that was still the hardest thing for me to separate in my mind: that the things that loomed out of the darkness like nightmares maybe weren't. And it wasn't just the propaganda that had been shoved down my throat since I was a kid, or even the fact that the Faceless had almost destroyed humanity a few generations ago. It was something on a deeper level than that. It was something instinctive. Primal. It was their faces, formless and blank because of their inky-black masks. It was because they were unknowable.

The Faceless watched us for a moment longer, and then moved away.

I fanned my cards out in my hand, and stared at them without really seeing. "Where are they taking us, do you think?"

"I don't know," Cam said softly. He smiled faintly. "You're not getting stir-crazy like Chris, are you?"

"I was born stir-crazy, LT," I reminded him. "But no, not really. I mean, it would be nice to know how long this will last, you know? Even back on Defender Three I at least had days to count down. I'm not good with just *being*, you know?"

Cam huffed out a breath at that, and I wondered if he was remembering the time intel threw us into a shared cell back home. "I know."

"Last night Doc asked me about my plans for the future," I said, unsure why I'd even let those words tumble out of me. My chest felt tight because of it. "He asked me what I wanted for myself, if I could have anything. Is it weird that I don't know?"

There was nothing in Cam's gaze but understanding. "I don't think that's weird."

"What will you do?" I asked him. "When we get home."

He showed me that soft smile again, which maybe had less to do with his own dreams and more to do with the fact that I was finally entertaining the idea we actually had a future. "I'll stay in the military, probably," he said.

I rolled my eyes. "Seriously?"

"For a while," he said. "When we get home, Brady, things are going to be different. Whatever happens, the military and the government are going to have to come up with a new approach to dealing with the Faceless. I'll see which way the wind is blowing, I guess, and see where I can do the most good. Maybe that's staying in the military, or maybe it's quitting and working for some government body. There are seven of us on this ship. When we get back, we're going to make sure our voices are heard."

"You're counting me and Lucy in that seven?" I snorted at that. "We're reffos, and she's a *kid*. And it sounds like you're counting on the idea that we'll actually learn something about the Faceless."

"We already have," Cam said. "When I was taken, it was unthinkable that I'd survive. And here we are. Voluntarily. It's a huge step forward, Brady. And it's messy and experimental, but can you imagine what it'll be like at home when they find out what we've done? When they find out we went with the Faceless, and came back unharmed?"

"They'll think we're traitors and hang us in the streets."

Cam shook his head, his eyes crinkling at the corners. "You have a very bleak view of humanity, don't you?"

"Yeah. It's called the voice of experience, asshole." I was only half-teasing, I think. "So you'll be part of some government department, probably flying to all sorts of exotic locations and dealing with officials from districts all over the world. What will I be?"

"Whatever you want," Cam said, like it was that simple.

"What if I want to hang around at our place all day just waiting for Lucy to get back from school?"

"Brady." His tone was suddenly serious. "Whatever you want."

"I'd get bored," I muttered.

"Then do it until you get bored," Cam said. "And then find something else to do."

It wouldn't be that simple. Even if we made it home—*when* we made it home—the military still owned my sorry ass. But six years of mopping floors suddenly didn't seem so bad. Cam and I had proved last time that we had at least some leverage over the brass. They'd let us live together even though fraternization between officers and enlisted men wasn't allowed. They'd let us bring Lucy down from Kopa, even though she was a reffo. And I'd hardly ever been thrown in the stockade, even given the number of times I'd mouthed off to someone I shouldn't have. And maybe Cam was right. Maybe this time we'd have even more leverage, which would translate to even more leeway.

Maybe I could even demand citizenship for me and Lucy, so that they couldn't just send us back to Kopa when my service ran out. Cam would probably find a way to swing it. Cam, and Doc, and maybe even Chris Varro. They were smart and more importantly they knew how to work the system. They didn't just get angry and punch walls when shit didn't go their way.

I could mop floors for six years if Lucy and I got citizenship out of it. And maybe I could use those six years to think of what I wanted to do after. I didn't have to know now. Maybe Doc thought I should have some sort of ambition burning inside me. Maybe he thought it was a waste that I didn't. But I'd meant what I'd told him. I was ahead of the curve, and not even mopping floors would change that.

"We're okay," Cam said. He drew another card from the stack. "You and me, and Lucy. And whatever happens, here or back home, we'll figure it out."

And he said it with such calm certainty that a part of me even believed it.

I studied the backs of Cam's cards for a while, trying to figure out exactly what he was holding. Found myself looking at his fingers more than the cards. Those steady hands of his. Just watching them made me want to lean forward into his touch. It made something in my chest ache.

"You're the bravest guy I ever met," I said, lifting my gaze to meet his. "Stepping foot on this ship again."

He drew his brows together, a faint line appearing at the top of his nose. He tilted his head. "Where's this coming from?"

I reached out and took his hand. Pressed it to my heart. "It's always in here, Cam. I just figured I should remember to say it sometimes too."

Cam drew me into an embrace and we sat there, our cards forgotten as stars slipped by the window and the Faceless took us deeper into the black.

CHAPTER 4

IN A DARK, dappled bay on the Faceless ship a row of pods lay on the damp floor. The pods shone like beetles' carapaces under the dull lights that slid through the membranous walls of the ship. The pods were large—big enough to fit a tall Faceless inside, and more than big enough to send an abducted human prisoner of war back through the vacuum of space to the nearest Defender. And they were big enough to have once held a scrawny human recruit whose bones had been snapped, whose ribs had been caved in, and whose lungs had been rapidly filling with blood.

Chris was fascinated by the pods—probably because he'd never been in one. He ran his fingers along the carapace and leaned over the edge so that he could see inside. The pods were empty. When they were in use they were filled with gross milky fluid that was held inside by a sac. Chris's fingers slid down the inside of the carapace, and I shivered.

The faint light gleamed on the stubbled planes of his face. "I can't even see any controls."

I thought of how I'd first seen Cam lying in a pod, corpse-white with illuminated characters scrolling along his skin.

Cam was in the room too, leaning against a nearby pod and wearing a faint smile on his face like he was dreaming of the hundred different things the pod had showed him when he was in it. I'd shared some of those memories of floating through the stars. I'd shared a pod with him once too, and we'd both blinked awake in a sun-drenched paddock in Kopa, insects buzzing in the grass around us and cockatoos screeching in the trees.

It had felt real.

It had felt so real that it sometimes made me worry that nothing was. That these moments now, and everything that had come before them, was nothing more than a virtual reality the pod had constructed for us. How could I be sure that it wasn't? How could I be sure that my entire life wasn't? How could I be sure that I wasn't just chained up in a cave, watching a shadow play on the walls?

There was a reason Doc didn't like me to read his philosophy books. Mostly because my brain got caught up in the nausea of nihilism and never could make the leap to the part that was supposed to be liberating. It was just the way I was built. I'd never been the sort of guy who, when he couldn't feel the ground beneath his feet, figured that he was flying. Plummeting maybe, but never flying.

And somehow I'd ended up with a fucking *pilot*.

I crossed over to Cam and leaned against the pod beside him. Wriggled a bit when his hand slid over my ass and into the back pocket of my pants. I looked to see if Chris was watching, but he was engrossed in his inspection of the pod like if he just stared at it hard enough it would somehow reveal all its secrets to him.

I tugged Cam's hand out of my pocket, linked my fingers through his, and led him out of the room.

I doubt Chris even noticed us go.

"He wants it to make sense, doesn't he?" I asked as we walked along a corridor that curved gently upward as it spiraled. "And it's not going to make sense."

Cam's brows drew together slightly. "I think that he wants to understand it in a way that he can explain to others. And I think that maybe that's never going to happen. The Faceless aren't something we can understand on that level. They're something we have to accept might be unknowable."

"There were probably cavemen once who thought that way about fire."

Cam's mouth quirked. "Oh, so you're on Chris's side now?"

"Nope. Because Chris won't ever think he's the caveman in this scenario." I held his gaze. "But some of this is your fault too."

"My fault?"

"When you came back talking about shit like battle regents, and treaties, and hierarchies. You lied, Cam. You made guys like Chris think we had some common ground or something."

Cam shrugged. "What was I supposed to say? Oh, the Faceless are almost entirely incomprehensible, but our creepy telepathic link gives me the impression that Kai-Ren couldn't be bothered killing us all?"

He had a point, but it went deeper than that too, I knew. I'd never really brought it up with him, but I knew. I wrinkled my nose. "So what's going to happen when we go home empty-handed?"

"We're not empty-handed," Cam said. "We still have a treaty, and we're here, alive. We're already doing something that most people on Earth think is impossible. Just because we might go back without knowing a thing about their tech or their weapons doesn't mean we're not laying the groundwork for an enduring peace."

"You really believe that?"

Cam nodded. "Yeah, I really do."

"You think that one day we'll build big cities again?" I'd seen pictures of them before. Cities so huge that they covered hundreds of square kilometers, lights burning so bright that the people who lived there must never have seen the night sky. And those bright burning cities, their networks of blazing lights visible even from way out in the black, had been nothing but targets for the Faceless.

Cities were smaller now.

Much smaller.

"Maybe," Cam said, and then smiled at the thought. "Why not?"

I couldn't quite wrap my head around the idea of that, but Cam was right: why not? My whole life my dreams had been small-drawn, and I'd never been able to get past that before, not even all the way out here, but today was a new day and so *why not?* Maybe in a generation or two, humanity could be back to where we were before the Faceless came. Maybe people would build those huge cities again, and remember what it was like to be unafraid of the black. And maybe we would never truly understand the Faceless, but we wouldn't have to fear them.

It should have been impossible, but what was impossible, anyway? Me and Cam, standing here onboard a Faceless ship—our hands clasped and our heartbeats steady—*that* should have been impossible.

Yet here we were.

"Look out, Cam," I murmured, leaning in close. "You might even turn me into an optimist."

He laughed, his breath warm against my cheek. "See? Nothing's impossible."

Yeah. I'd been slow on the uptake, like always, but maybe I was finally starting to get that.

I STILL HAD those dreams sometimes at night. The ones where I was back in Cam's head—in Cam's body—and I was a prisoner of the Faceless. I was restrained, naked, and Kai-Ren raped me.

Cam didn't like that word. He didn't like to look it in the face. He made excuses for it, for them, as though I couldn't feel the exact same terror that he had. He rationalized it—the Faceless weren't like us, the Faceless didn't know what rape was and wouldn't understand even if they did—but changing the word didn't change what had happened. Cam pretended that it did, pretended that it had been worth it because it had facilitated the bond between him and Kai-Ren, as though that bond hadn't been forged in pain and terror and hurt.

He still had nightmares too.

Sometimes I wondered if the only way he'd even held himself together when the Faceless had sent him back to Defender Three was because he'd thought he wouldn't last a day. That he'd be shot in the head and thrown out the nearest airlock. And instead they'd locked him in a room with a smartass trainee medic who had literally shared his dreams.

There was this guy once, back in Kopa, whose missus drowned their kids in the creek and then hanged herself from a tree on the bank. They found her swinging there hours later, the rope creaking in the breeze. And for a while everyone kept a close eye on the guy, because he wasn't some asshole or anything. Then, later, it was like he got better. He wasn't angry anymore, or drinking, or screaming. He was back to normal, everyone thought, right up until he climbed to the roof of the foundry after work one day, and then jumped off it.

I sometimes wondered if that had been Cam, back on Defender Three. Calm and quiet and rational, because in his mind the ground was already rushing up to meet him and there was nothing he could do to stop it. I'd never had the courage to ask him though, and I probably never would.

But at night, when his mouth pressed into a hard, thin line that still couldn't keep all his noises in, and when his body shook with the things that Kai-Ren did to him, I held him tight and I wondered.

The nights were sometimes rough but the days passed with the tick-tick-tick of Doc's wind-up clock. They passed with drawing pictures with Lucy, with pop quizzes on anatomy, and with the stars out in the black slipping slowly past the windows.

And then one day it changed, with a tendril of color painted faintly across the black, and then another and another as it built up like a coming storm. Clouds slid by instead of stars, and they grew thicker and thicker like a rolling fog. Pink and orange and green and purple; the clouds smothered the stars until they were all that we could see. It felt almost claustrophobic. Lucy crowed with delight at all the beautiful colors and I listened to Harry telling her about emission nebulas and interstellar clouds and ionized gasses and photons and wavelengths.

Fuck if I knew what he was talking about, but I'd never been able to wrap my head around any of that bullshit. All I knew was that there was a point where light and time smashed together, and that looking at a distant star was exactly the same as looking back in time, and then my brain filled up with static and I was done.

The clouds swirled by outside and reminded me of this one time when I was a kid and this circus came to Kopa. It wasn't much, probably. Just a dusty vinyl tent that trapped the heat inside, and flags hanging limply from the ropes, but some of the kids from the school said that there would be ponies and monkeys. My dad didn't have the money to buy me a ticket so I did what most of the other kids did: hung around the tent and stared at all the people going inside. There were trucks selling food and fizzy drinks too. And in one of them, a man who was making fairy floss: stirring it through and through like he was catching clouds on a stick. Sometimes he made them all one color, but the rainbow ones were my favorite. One of the other kids bought one, and tore some off for me to try.

We weren't always selfish, the poor kids like me. But sometimes, when you got a good thing, you wanted to keep it all for yourself. You wanted to hold it tight like a secret so that nobody could take it away.

"Don't tell the others," the kid warned me, his eyes big. "Don't tell."

"I won't!" I think I was probably small enough that I crossed my heart and everything. Small enough and dumb enough back then that a promise from me still meant something.

Looking out at the swirling clouds of color, I could almost taste the sugar on my lips, and I wondered what that kid was doing now.

I hoped he was okay.

OUR IMMERSION into the nebula brought about a strange shift of mood aboard the Faceless ship. There was a prickling sense of something coming off the Faceless, that felt a little like anticipation. They seemed more alert somehow, more invested in our surroundings. One morning I passed two of them standing by a window, watching the clouds swirl by, and I couldn't think of a time that the Faceless had ever been more interested in the view than in one of us humans.

"Something's happening," Chris said that day at lunch, his notebook tucked under his arm as he dug into one of our last remaining ration packs. "There's a lot more activity amongst the Faceless. And the temperature is getting warmer too. Cam, will you talk to Kai-Ren? He takes the time to answer you."

It was said without rancor, but it had to smart a bit, right?

I ducked my head to hide my grin. When I looked up again, Chris was watching me, his expression unreadable.

"Okay," Cam said. "We'll talk to him."

But he made no move to get up, and Chris looked at him expectantly.

"Now?" Cam asked, raising his eyebrows.

Chris shrugged. "Do you have anything more pressing to do today?"

"I guess not," Cam said, and he sounded more amused than annoyed. The canvas of the bunk squeaked as he stood.

I stared at Chris for a moment longer, trying to figure out if his tone had been teasing, or if he was being a prick. And then I tried to figure out why it felt like something that mattered even though Cam didn't seem bothered.

I didn't know whether I wanted to laugh, or whether I wanted to punch him. Cam must have sensed it.

"Come on, Brady," he said, slapping me on the back. "Let's go."

I shot Chris a narrow look as I followed Cam from the room.

"Was he always such a dick?" I muttered under my breath as we headed down the corridor.

"Sometimes," Cam said with a slight smile. "Not always. Come on, we'll go and talk to Kai-Ren and see what's going on. Then you can rub it in Chris's face."

I snorted, but Cam was right.

Humanity was very much beneath Kai-Ren's attention, but Cam and I stood out just a little bit more than the other buzzing insects. Cam, because he'd been the first, and me because I'd been so different from Cam. That had snagged Kai-Ren's attention, and still held it for the most part. Kai-Ren humored us, but it only went so far. Fuck, I didn't know. Most days it felt like he ignored us, but for all I knew he'd told us everything we'd ever wanted to know about the Faceless and we just had no way of understanding. Maybe every hiss, every touch, and every frisson of shared emotion was brimming with information that our primitive human brains just had no way to process. Talking to us was probably like trying to explain quantum mechanics to a housecat.

There was no bridge on the Faceless ship, or operations center or anything like that, just like there was no mess, no crew quarters, and no rec rooms. But there was a section of the ship towards the core where the alcoves with flashing lights were more concentrated and the twisting roots of the ship's architecture were thicker and closer together, that we might have considered a bridge if we'd actually known what the alcoves did. The Faceless tended to gather there.

Cam and I followed the sloping spiral of the corridor downward and listened for that peculiar humming in our skulls where our consciousnesses touched those of the Faceless. It was like hearing cicadas in the distance, or the faint crackle of static between two radio channels.

Chris was right about the temperature. The ship was more humid now than it had been before, like summer nights in Kopa, twisted in thin sheets, skin slick with sweat. Too hot to sleep, lying awake and listening to the high-pitched drone of mosquitoes that drifted just out of reach. Windows pushed open in the hopes of a breath of cool air, but there was nothing but cloud-pressed heat, still and heavy. If I closed my eyes I might have been in Kopa, with the salt taste of sweat beading on my upper lip, and my shirt stuck to my back.

Halfway across the universe, and it was closest to home I'd felt in a long time.

Lights pulsed in the walls as we followed the corridor down into the heart of the ship, and the humming chorus that was the shared consciousness of the Faceless washed up against our own. It always brought a moment of wrongness, a faint psychic scrape in the back of my skull like a nail against a chalkboard. It was just enough to make my flesh prickle, but it vanished again in the space of a heartbeat.

We passed one of the Faceless, and then another.

They all looked the same under their sleek black body armor, like insects in a hive, but we could tell them apart now, or at least tell which one was Kai-Ren. It was chemosignals, maybe, because we were insects in the hive as well now, weren't we? We weren't just observers anymore. Maybe we never had been.

We found Kai-Ren in an alcove lit with muted orange lights that flickered back and forth through the veins in the ceiling. He loomed over us, his shining black suit reflecting the lights. "Camren. Bray-dee."

He reached out, and his black-gloved fingers slid along my collarbone, where the neck of my T-shirt sagged and gaped. I felt his interest sharpen as he touched my skin and found it damp with sweat. Then his fingertips snagged on the fabric of my shirt as he sought out my heartbeat with his palm.

"Where are we?" Cam asked him.

Kai-Ren turned his face toward him. As always he spoke in a hissing burst of sounds that no human should have been able to understand. Those sounds were translated by the connection that bound our consciousness to the hive's. "We are home."

Cam's confusion was a flicker of static, and mental pictures of the things he'd seen the last time he'd been with the Faceless. The two suns. The purple sky. The towers that reached up to touch it, bulging with cupolas and buttresses like the massive nests of cathedral termites. "This isn't the place you took me to the first time."

"Home," Kai-Ren said again, his voice skipping as the connection lagged and then over-compensated. We heard the words, but an outsider who didn't share the connection only would have heard those hissing sounds. "This is where we are from. Where we are made. Only here."

I blinked, and saw a flash of color in my vision, like for a moment the interstellar clouds outside the ship had somehow been projected onto the inside of my eyelids.

"I don't understand," Cam said, his eyebrows drawing together, and I wondered if he'd seen the same thing. If, several decks above us in our room, through the membranous passages and conduits and walls of the ship, everyone else had too. "Kai-Ren, I don't understand."

And that was the kicker, right? And it always would be. We just didn't understand. We couldn't force our mouths to move in the right way to even make the same sound the Faceless used to name their species. Kai-Ren had broken down the barriers between our minds and it still wasn't enough for understanding. But we all kept trying, didn't we? Chris, and Cam, and even me, in my own stupid way.

I looked up at Kai-Ren's Faceless mask now, like somehow, even after all this time, I expected to find the answers there.

Nothing but dark space.

A slow learner, my stepmother always used to call me. She was probably right.

If Kai-Ren was even staring back at me, I had no way of knowing.

Kai-Ren made a humming noise as my heart thumped under his palm, and then he lifted his hand from my chest. "Come."

He leaned back into the wall of the alcove, and it melted around him. For a moment the shape of him was illuminated by the pulsing orange lights, and he looked like some sort of sea creature, a jellyfish swimming in a dark ocean, and then he was gone.

Cam took my hand, drew a breath, and we followed Kai-Ren into the walls of the ship.

The fluid hurt my eyes—a saltwater sting—and then it was gone. Noise vanished with it, and became muted and low. My chest ached as I held my breath for longer than I should have and then, my muscles tensing with the knowledge of what was coming next, I opened my mouth and the fluid flooded in.

There was always a moment of panic when my lungs first pulled in fluid instead of air, a moment where I wanted to claw at my throat and choke. But it lasted for seconds at most, and then it passed, leaving nothing but a strange heaviness in my chest, the memory of an ache, and my lizard brain's silent, primeval screech in the back of my skull that this wasn't natural and that I was going to asphyxiate. It always took a moment to shut that asshole up. He'd been screaming that at me since I first stepped on board a shitbox and left the Earth's atmosphere.

A moment of disquiet always followed the panic: we were putting something *alien* in our bodies, and we didn't even know what was in it. This one was easier to smother that the panic, because after everything that had gone before, what the hell did it matter?

I exhaled and opened my eyes, my lungs spasming reflexively as they adjusted, and bubbles rose in front of my face. The liquid in the walls was warm, heavier than water. It was thick and viscous like amniotic fluid, and, from what we could tell, carried enough oxygen and nutrients to keep us alive, as well as something that accelerated our healing if we were injured or sick. We could live on it if we had to, and once our supplies ran all the way out I guessed we would.

It was gross, but it was better than starving to death.

This wasn't one of the alcoves we'd been shown to feed in though. This was a wall, and Kai-Ren had already stepped through it and was waiting for us on the other side.

We followed him through, the wall melting and reforming around us seamlessly.

Coming out was always worse than going in. My lungs burned

as I coughed and hacked the fluid up and drew a sharp, painful breath that felt like a knife in the chest. It took a moment before I could stand upright again, and before I could clear the fluid out of my eyes and take a look around.

We were standing in a large, vaulted chamber. It was dark apart from the lights shifting in the walls, and the air was dense and moist. It was hotter in here than in the rest of the ship. There were no doors into the room, hence coming through the walls, and no windows to the outside or through to other rooms. In the middle of the floor there was what looked to be a shallow pool, with thick, membranous sides keeping the liquid contained. It was a little raised from the floor, and a strange haze hung over it like a fog. It took me a moment to realize it was steam. The strange muddy fluid in the pool was so hot it was almost at boiling point.

Kai-Ren stood at the side of the pool, and Cam and I moved forward to join him.

"Here is home," Kai-Ren said, and made a protracted hissing sound that didn't translate in our minds. A flash of something that felt like frustration buzzed between us, and then he tried again. "Here is where we begin."

He reached into the simmering liquid of the pool, not even flinching as his hand sank up to the wrist and he withdrew a drooping sac. He cupped it in his gloved hands and held it out to show us.

"Here is where we make a hive."

A strange, tiny thing flicked and flicked and flicked beneath the opaque skin of the sac, and for a moment I didn't understand what I was looking at.

And then, in a sudden rush, I did.

That flickering little movement, as rapid as the beating wings of an insect, was a pulse. A tiny muscle throbbing in a still-forming embryo.

A heart.

A *life*.

We were in a Faceless hatchery, and Kai-Ren was showing us one of their young.

This was where the Faceless began.

I'd thought of them as insects, hadn't I? Ever since the beginning, I'd thought of them as cold-blooded creatures in a hive. The only thing missing was the queen.

I stared down at the tick-tick-ticking heartbeat of the sac held in Kai-Ren's hands. Behind him, the walls pulsed in the same rhythm.

And then I realized.

Hadn't I also thought from the beginning that the ship was a living thing? The ship wasn't the hive. The ship was the queen, and we were all living inside her.

CHAPTER 5

THE COLORFUL CLOUDS of the nebula washed past in our slip-stream and painted my skin faintly green with the light that filtered through the window. I missed daylight. I missed the burn of sunlight on my back. I blinked my eyes a few times to try to clear my vision, but nothing happened.

It was hot. I sweated and itched and my shirt stuck to my back. I stank, probably, but so did we all.

I watched as Harry walked over to the wall. He lifted his hand to touch it, and his brow furrowed. He dropped his hand back to his side again, his fingers twitching.

He didn't want to touch the inside of the queen with his fingers, and meanwhile his bare feet were leaving damp prints on the floor. Meanwhile whatever fluids she produced were keeping him alive. Meanwhile he was living inside her like a parasite, sucking at her like a tick getting bloated with her blood.

Harry's fingers shook as he shoved his hand inside his pocket, and the rush of nausea I felt might have been all mine, or it might have been feedback from the connection we shared.

A glob of something, dark and shapeless like a clot, slid through the walls.

Harry looked away, his mouth turning down.

I swallowed and tasted bile in the back of my throat. Nothing had changed today except our perception but sometimes that was all it took. We were all shaken. Doc looked greener around the gills than the light necessitated and even Andre looked a little faint.

Chris was the only adult in the room who didn't seem to be bothered by the idea that the Faceless ship might be an insect queen. He was standing over Cam, watching intently as Cam drew a sketch of the weird pool in the hatchery in Chris's ubiquitous notebook.

Lucy was drawing too, sitting on the bunk beside me with her legs swinging. She was drawing rainbow clouds that looked like fairy floss. She was wearing one of the gray pinafores they'd made for her back on Defender Three. She was hunched over so that it gaped a little at the front and the braces took turns sliding off her skinny shoulders. Her shoulder blades were sharp as wings.

They wouldn't know us now on Defender Three. We went barefoot most days, and shirtless in the heat. Doc had even cut off a pair of pants at the knees to wear them as shorts, his hairy legs bristling out the ends. None of us would pass muster by military standards these days. Most days I wondered if we'd forgotten how to be military. Days like today I wondered if we were forgetting how to be human too.

The Faceless had already changed us once, with the connection between us. What if it didn't end there? We breathed the humid air inside the queen. We ingested whatever was in the fluids that flowed in her veins. What if exposure meant mutation?

"I need a cigarette," Doc muttered, slipping from the room.

I followed that siren call, and rounded the corner into his makeshift medbay.

"I don't fucking have any," he grumbled at me, like it was my fault. "But I'd give my left nut for one right about now."

"Thought I was on a promise," I said, and sat down on one of the plastic crates he used to keep his books from getting damp.

Doc sighed. He reached for his little wind-up clock. His surgeon's hands shook as he turned the wheel on the back. "Well," he said, gruff as always, "that was some unsettling shit you and Rushton shared just now."

I shifted my weight where I sat. Behind me, the walls of the living ship pulsed. "Right?"

"It's a good theory though," he said, his bushy eyebrows tugging together. "It's solid. Maybe the ship has to come here for the temperature to be right for the embryos to grow, or for the eggs to be fertilized, or whatever the hell is needed to kickstart them."

"Radiation, maybe," I suggested.

"Maybe," Doc said, setting the clock aside. "There's literally nothing off the table at this point, is there?"

That was what made it so unsettling, I figured. There were no certainties here. No truths. There was no solid ground underneath our feet when it came to the Faceless. We were just spinning in space, untethered, like always.

Doc tugged a pen out of his pocket and jammed it between his teeth. He chewed on it aggressively for a moment. "What's Varro going to make of it, I wonder?"

"Chris?" I wrinkled my nose. "What do you mean?"

"He's from intel, son," Doc reminded me. "And Kai-Ren just told us where to find the ship's hatchery. You think a man who's spend the last three months looking for weapons isn't going to think about that tactical advantage?"

"Doesn't matter," I said, unease biting at me all the same. "We've got nothing."

"We've got information," Doc corrected me. "We just learned more about the Faceless today than we have in months. We learned where they keep their young, and we learned that this place, this cloud—whatever the fuck it is—is necessary for the breeding process. Do you remember why we don't put women on Defenders, Brady?"

"Yeah." I chewed my lip for a moment. "Because women are more important than men when it comes to keeping a species alive."

"Don't make that face," Doc said with a growl. "You know how it works. It's a numbers game, pure and simple. If you have one man and fifty women, in nine months you can have fifty babies. But if you have one woman and fifty men, in nine months you'll only have one baby." He shrugged. "Generally speaking."

"Yeah, so you don't put your most valuable resource on the front line," I said, and thought of Lucy, and my mother, and my ex-girlfriend Kaylee. I thought of all the women who lived in Kopa, their faces lined by the time they were in their twenties, red dust ground into their cracked skin. Nobody was worth anything much in Kopa. Not men, not women, and not kids. All that talk about the future of humanity, about women being precious resources, but reffos weren't a part of that equation. It was life and death for humanity, caught between the Faceless and extinction, and we still found a way to make shit like where you were from matter.

Doc nodded, his gaze fixed on me as he chewed his pen. "So if, this place, this cloud, really is the only place the Faceless can breed? Kai-Ren just brought us right to it."

I was slow on the uptake. "What's that got to do with Chris?"

"He'd be a fool," Doc said, "not to think about some way to use that against them."

My stomach twisted. "Are you serious, Doc?"

He shrugged. "Brady, I'm a doctor. My whole fucking thing is about the preservation of life, and *I'm* thinking it. What are the chances those boys from intel aren't already ten steps ahead of me?"

"He just wants to understand them, doesn't he?" I thought back to every memory I'd shared of Chris's. He burned to know things, to understand. He was the one who'd cooked up this crazy plan to connect with the Faceless voluntarily. But Doc was right. He'd be a fool not to consider all his options, and Chris was no fool. "I mean, he'll be considering it, for what it's worth, but we don't have any weapons. We couldn't put a dent in a Faceless ship with the tech that we have. We sure as fuck couldn't blow up their breeding grounds. Do you know what nuclear weapons do in space?"

"Do you?" Doc asks, the hint of a teasing smile tugging at his mouth.

"Course I don't." I rolled my eyes. "But fuck all, probably. It'd be like throwing a water bomb in the fucking ocean."

"Exactly," Doc said. "But we're surrounded by Faceless tech, aren't we?"

"Faceless tech we can't use."

"Yet," Doc said, and spat out a tiny piece of chewed plastic. It hit the damp floor, and then sank into it and was subsumed. "We can't use it *yet*."

Okay.

Okay, yeah, so that was probably what Doc meant by Chris being ten steps ahead, because of course he would have considered options I didn't even think of.

"You think he's planning something?" I asked, lowering my voice.

"I dunno, son," Doc said. There was a dark blue mark on his lip from where he'd split the pen open. "It's big, you know? And intel doesn't train diplomats."

Yeah.

I shrugged though, because what difference did it make?

So maybe Chris was ten steps ahead of guys like me and Doc. But what the fuck did that matter when he was still a thousand steps behind the Faceless? A thousand steps behind the Faceless, and a million miles from home.

THE CANVAS of Cam's bunk creaked, and a moment later he was climbing in beside me. I blinked my eyes open to discover that the light filtering through the window was blue now. It settled on the planes of Cam's face and made him look sick and washed-out like some consumptive patient with one foot already in the grave. I missed seeing his skin under sunlight, and kissing him when he tasted like saltwater from the wind that whipped off the ocean.

I kissed him now, still half asleep, and shifted to make room for him. I rested one hand on his hip, my fingers brushing against the humidity-damp fabric of his underwear, and my thumb resting against his skin. He slipped a leg between mine, the rasp of our hair bringing me out in goose bumps, and then we kissed again.

It wasn't leading anywhere. Not in a room full of other guys, with my little sister sleeping in the bunk right above mine. Just because they'd been in our heads once and seen all our memories didn't mean they got a free show now.

"You were quiet tonight," Cam murmured, his breath hot on my lips. "You feeling okay?"

He knew I wasn't, of course. I was pretty sure I'd been transmitting a discordant note of unease through our connection since I'd spoken to Doc.

"Just a lot I'm thinking about," I told him. "With all this new Faceless stuff."

"Yeah." He bumped our noses together. "Don't think too hard, okay?"

I snorted and closed my eyes. "Okay."

Sometimes I didn't want the universe to be any bigger than this. Just Cam and me, skin and heartbeats. Sometimes I wished that time would just stop in moments like these and we'd remain this way forever like insects caught in amber. That was the pessimist in me talking, or maybe the realist. Because if everything was in a state of decay, if the balance of the universe always tipped towards entropy, then how long could Cam and I stand against those odds? Every day we were together, weren't we also another day closer to ruin? But wasn't every day we were together also another day I wouldn't give up for anything?

That was the difference between me and Cam, I think. He took every day as a gift. I took every day as one step closer to the end. And I was trying to flip that around, trying to be more like him, but maybe I didn't have that capacity for optimism in me. Maybe the glass was never going to be half full for someone like me.

"You..." Cam stroked the side of my face, his touch drawing my eyes open again. "I love you."

Such quiet certainty in his tone.

"I love you too," I whispered back, and that was the core of both our very different universes at least; the truth around which everything else orbited like a boiling sun.

Cam smiled, and pressed his mouth against mine again. The kiss was faint and fleeting and I tilted my chin up to chase down another one when the first ended. And another, open-mouthed, our tongues touching softly, the heat building slowly between us. Cam's body shook with a silent laugh as I rocked my hips, and his hand slid down the back of my underwear.

Maybe we both wanted to take it further, but also neither of us wanted to move it outside, so laziness won out against nascent arousal in the end and we settled and breathed slow and deep.

The strange blue light washed over the walls, over our skin, and for once I tried just to look at the color of it, and not think of radiation and mutation and cancerous cells dividing endlessly inside us. But it was impossible to think we'd come back from out here unscathed, wasn't it? Impossible to think that there wouldn't be an ugly price to pay.

Blue light caught on Cam's lips as they quirked. "Didn't I say not to think too hard?"

"Yeah." I released a long breath. "I'm trying."

"I know." His hand settled on the base of my spine.

I closed my eyes again, and pretended that we were all that existed in the universe.

"I've got you," he murmured. "I've got you, Brady."

He held me as I drifted off into sleep.

I DREAMED of home that night. I dreamed of red dirt underneath my bare feet and sunlight burning my shoulders. I dreamed of the taste of salt on my cracked lips, and the heavy smell of mudflats and mangroves on every hot breath of wind. I dreamed of my dad's voice, and of his hands. His fingers, long and dexterous, as he stirred sugar into a cup of tea. I dreamed of his careworn face with lines on it that belonged on a much older man. I dreamed of the calluses on his palms, the gray in his hair, and the shadows, dark as bruises, under his eyes. I dreamed of his smile.

I dreamed I walked through our house—it had more rooms in the dream than it did in reality; a never-ending maze of them, a twisting labyrinth—and I could hear Dad's voice but I couldn't find him. He was always just a room away. I caught glimpses of his shadow, but I couldn't catch him. In my dream I panicked and got scared. I started to run, but he was always out of reach. Just a room away, but it might have been an entire universe.

"Brady?" A warm touch on my face brought me around. Cam's thumb sliding across my tear-damp cheek. His fingers cupping the hinge of my jaw. "You were having a bad dream."

I lay still for a moment, letting my eyes slide shut again so that I didn't have to see if anyone else was awake and watching. "Yeah."

Cam slid his hand to my chest, and my heartbeat thumped against his palm. Echoed in my mind a little, in the connection between us, and I thought of the Faceless hatchery, of all the fluid-filled sacs, of all those tiny hearts pumping as fast as the beat of an insect's wings. Maybe someone else would have looked at those things in the hatchery and seen a miracle. Maybe Cam did, but not me. It make my skin crawl.

"I'm not made for this," I whispered into the darkness. "Not made for expanding horizons."

He rubbed his palm in a circle over my chest. "Maybe nobody is."

It was a lie, but a nice one.

"I need a cigarette," I said at last, and pushed Cam away. I sat up and swung my legs over the edge of the cot. The soles of my feet met the warm, damp floor. The flesh of the living creature we infested like parasites. Could it feel us, burrowing in like hookworms?

Bile rose in my throat.

I didn't have any cigarettes but that didn't stop me from going through my footlocker, twice, hoping that maybe I'd missed one the last time I'd searched it.

The light outside was reddish now, like the faint glow from a dying campfire, and I thought of embers that floated up into a starlit night. I missed the feeling of dirt under my feet. Missed the smell of the air from home. Such small things, really, but without them I was unanchored and adrift in a churning black sea that I didn't understand.

I was out here now, facing my fears, and maybe finding myself a little braver than I'd ever imagined, but I was still homesick. That wouldn't ever go away, probably. I'd only ever had small-drawn dreams, but it turns out they were harder to reach than the stars. And that was okay, maybe. That was just life, maybe. Because if I was finding myself braver than I'd ever thought, then I'd also gone much farther than anyone would ever have imagined someone like me would. And maybe that even counted for something in the end.

I sat back on my heels and looked over the room. Cam was watching me—I sensed it more than saw it in the weird, dim light —and one or two more consciousness prickled against mine like faint static. Andre and Chris. They were awake too.

I climbed to my feet and left the room.

It was darker in the corridor, and quiet. I closed my eyes for a moment and waited to feel the Faceless in my mind. Waited for my synapses to map them. There was one close by, feeding in the walls. The rest were closer to the core of the ship. Kai-Ren was down there too—magnetic north on the compass he planted in my brain.

I wondered what Chris and the others had thought this would be. Translation and negotiation, maybe. Cultures clashing before discovering shared ground. We had a term for that on Earth, didn't we? Common humanity. It was meant to encompass everyone, but the limitations of it were right there in the words. The Faceless were too alien. Cam had tried to be an emissary once, a bridge between us and the Faceless. He'd tried to translate them into ways that we would understand, and into ways that meant he didn't have to look what Kai-Ren did to him in the face—but the Faceless weren't like us. Not in any ways that mattered. Not in any ways that could be bridged. If Cam hadn't managed it, then how could anyone?

Kai-Ren had saved me, had saved all of us, but not because he understood us. Not because he thought we were worth anything. He'd saved us because our pain, our rage, our sorrow, our love—a maelstrom of muddied emotions screaming out into the black— had caught his attention like a glittering lure on a wire and he'd snapped it up like a fish.

I moved down the corridor, following a glowing glob of something that floated inside the walls.

Cam called me a pessimist, and maybe I was, but also maybe the reason I couldn't just bow and scrape to the almighty Faceless gods who held my life in their hands was that I was also a stubborn little asshole and always had been. Cam had put aside his pride and his ego for Kai-Ren because he was smarter than me, and because he was always thinking ahead to tomorrow. Not me though. Never me.

I drew a breath and remembered my stepmother Linda, and how she'd flogged the shit out of me for stealing from her and for talking back. Didn't stop me though, did it? Because all I had in me was that anger, burning like a flame. I refused to bend. I always broke instead.

I followed the curving corridor a short way down and turned into Doc's makeshift medbay.

Back on Defender Three on nights when my anger and fear wouldn't let me sleep, I'd head out of my barracks room and find some card game going on somewhere. Get drunk, maybe win some money, but probably lose some. If that didn't work I'd find someone else who was also itching for trouble, and rile him up until we fought. I'd been rattling the bars of my cage since the day I was born, probably, and I'd tried so hard to let go of my anger, of my pride, I'd tried so hard to not be that guy, but he kept coming back like a bad rash, didn't he?

I took one of Doc's books from the locker on the floor, and sat near a window to read it.

Doc had been trying to knock me into shape since the day he met me. He still was, so at least I wasn't the only one of us banging my head against that metaphorical wall over and over again. We all had windmills to tilt at, I guess, because we were all fucking crazy.

Maybe that's why the Faceless would never really understand us. They were a hive mind, or a machine where each component worked together to complete a task. We were a pack of feral dogs, growling and snapping at each other's tails.

I read a few pages of the book, and then looked up to see Cam leaning in the doorway.

"You want to talk about it?" he asked me softly.

"You're in my head," I said. "What's the fucking point?"

He didn't answer that, because, yeah, what was the fucking point?

I sighed and put the book away. "You remember on Defender Three when I looked after you?"

His mouth curled into a faint smile. "Yeah."

"I liked that," I said. "I liked when I felt important. When I felt like you needed me."

"I do need you, Brady," he said softly. "I always need you."

I knew that. I *felt* that. Cam's love was like a gold thread twisted through the connections that bound me to Lucy, to Doc, to Chris and Harry and Andre, to the Faceless. I could always feel it there, a guide rope through a dark room, or the chain of an anchor laying on the sea floor.

"I'm not useful here," I said, my voice cracking. "I'm not, Cam."

He closed the distance between us. "You are to me. I couldn't do this without you, Brady. I couldn't do any of this. I was lost out there, and I opened my eyes, and I saw you. You saved me. You brought me back."

I looked away, my chest aching.

Cam took me by the hand and drew me over to the narrow cot that Doc kept in here. He lay down, pulling me with him.

"Doc will get pissed if we fuck on his cot."

Cam snorted. "We're not going to fuck on his cot, Brady. Jesus."

"You fucking tease then."

"Shut up." Cam's smile was beautiful, and faded as slowly as a sunset. He shifted on the cot so that he was lying on his back and I was tucked up against his side. "You remember that first day on Defender Three? In the shower?"

"Mmm."

"You looked after me," Cam said. "I didn't know you. I was in shock, I think. I was so cold, and everything was loud, and I didn't know where I was, but you were there. This cute kid with eyes as big as an owl's, and you cleaned me up, and you talked to me. Do you remember what you told me?"

I shook my head. Bullshit, probably. It's what I usually talked, but Doc had always said I had a decent bedside manner.

"You told me your name," Cam said. "You told me where I was. And you told me all about the shitty ration packs and the asshole officers, and how some prick called Hooper owed you cigarettes from a card game."

"Still does, the fucker," I murmured.

"And I was *home*, Brady," Cam said, stroking my hair. "I was with humans again, and this kid was talking to me like I belonged there. And I knew I wasn't in the pod anymore. I knew I couldn't be, because how would my brain ever cobble together someone like you?"

"I'm going to take that as a compliment."

"You should," Cam said with a soft smile. He rubbed his thumb over the nape of my neck, the gentle contact making my skin prickle. "We help each other, Brady. We always have. You just don't see it because for some crazy reason you think I've actually got my shit together."

"So you're really a fuck up like me?" My eyes stung a little.

"Totally," Cam said, his smile growing.

"Liar," I whispered to him.

We lay quietly for a while. I closed my eyes, feeling like maybe sleep was in reach at last.

Cam shifted underneath me. "What's that?"

I opened my eyes to a kaleidoscope of shifting colored lights on the wall. And in the centre of them, a dark shadow that was growing larger.

We climbed off the cot and crossed to the window.

There, against the background of the green and red and blue clouds of the nebula, was dark space.

It was a Faceless ship, black and vast, and it was swallowing the light as it moved towards us.

CHAPTER 6

BY THE NEXT morning there were more of the Faceless ships in view, sometimes moving up close beside us, and sometimes falling back into our slipstream. Sometimes they vanished from view altogether, but they always reappeared again through the billowing colors of the nebula like fish chasing a lure through cloudy water.

"It's an armada," Chris said as he stared out the window in our room. "I can see at least four."

"Don't call it that," Cam said from where he was sitting on his footlocker with an open notebook on his knee and a pencil in his hand. He was sketching, I think. "Armada means a military fleet, and that's not what this is."

Chris turned back long enough to shoot him an amused look. "It's a bunch of ships, isn't it?"

"It's not an armada," Cam repeated.

"You're being pedantic," Chris said, like it was somehow his place to call Cam on it even if it had been true. I think that lit the spark of anger in me more than anything else.

"Fuck you," I said from my bunk. "Cam's right and you know it."

"Okay," Andre said. "Lucy, want to come visit Doc with me?"

Harry took the chance to escape with them.

"Oh," Chris said, turning back and folding his arms over his chest. "I'm about to get a lesson in linguistics from you, am I, Brady?"

"It's not an armada," I said, "because they're not ships. We call them that, but we're wrong. They're living things. It's a *herd*."

I felt a thrum of warmth from Cam at that, and I glanced over at him to see the quirk of his mouth as he ducked his head.

"If our ship is here to hatch its eggs, then so are theirs," I said.

Chris snorted at that because, yeah, there was no way of knowing. But it was as good a guess as anything else, and we were working entirely on guesswork out here.

"You're an expert now, are you?" Chris asked with a smirk.

"As much as you are." I leaned back on my bunk. "You can try and lord it over me all you want, Chris, but there's no fucking rank here, is there? There's just you and me and the fact that I'm fucking your ex-boyfriend on the regular."

He didn't bite, the asshole. Just smirked some more. "You still hung up on that? Are you worried he's comparing us and you just don't measure up?"

"He measures up," Cam said mildly.

Chris rolled his eyes, and I flashed a grin at Cam.

"Brady's right," Cam said. "It's a herd. You're thinking like a soldier, Chris, and it narrows your focus. If you really want to come anywhere near understanding the Faceless, you need to get rid of your preconceptions first."

"From the guy who called Kai-Ren a *battle regent*." Chris shook his head.

"I did what I had to do." Cam closed his notebook. "I explained him to you in terms that you'd relate to, and I'm not sorry for that. It was necessary and it worked. But the picture's gotten bigger since then."

Chris snorted. "You were always a good liar."

Cam held his gaze. "You had your moments too."

Chris glared at him for a moment, and then walked out of the room.

Cam returned to his notebook, and I watched him.

I'd always figured Chris was jealous of me for being with Cam, but maybe I'd misread that, or maybe it wasn't his only jealousy. He was jealous of Cam too, I realized now, because Cam had been the one taken by the Faceless and then returned. He knew exactly what Kai-Ren had done to Cam, and he was still jealous because Cam knew more than him. Because Cam had seen the bigger picture long before Chris had even guessed there was one. I wondered if it made me a hypocrite for hating him for that, when Cam himself wouldn't admit what happened to him gave him nightmares.

What was the difference between repressing something and letting it go? Like I could fucking tell. I'd never done either one in my entire life.

I opened my mouth.

"He's not an asshole," Cam said.

"I wasn't going to say that."

Cam raised his eyebrows. "I don't need to be in your head to read you like a book, Brady."

Okay, so maybe I was going to call him an asshole. I flopped back down on my bunk and fiddled with my dog tags. I don't even know why I still wore them. Habit, probably. They were as useless out here as anything else the military had given us, but I was accustomed to the feel of them.

"I can't figure him out," I said at last, thinking back to the conversation I'd had with Doc. Did it matter if Chris was thinking like a tactician? We were like apes with pointy sticks compared to the Faceless.

"He's not your enemy," Cam said. "There doesn't always have to be an enemy."

"If you think that, you're just not being creative enough."

That won an unwilling smile out of him. "You'd start a war with some guy who took the last pudding cup from the mess hall, wouldn't you?"

"Don't talk about pudding cups. Jesus, I'd kill for a pudding cup right now."

"You get my point though."

"Yeah." I twirled my dog tags. "I get your point."

Doc once told me that my bad attitude was my worst enemy, and he was probably right. When I was a kid I tried to make friends with this stray dog that was hanging around the town. I thought I could tame it but it never did stop growling and snapping. Made me wonder if Cam was betting against my nature in the same dumb way. Like he thought that maybe one day my first instinct wouldn't be to snarl and bite. And I'd worked on it real hard back home, with Cam's parents, and with Lucy's school, and with our landlord and everyone I was supposed to play nice with, to play normal with, to act like I was a real boy, but sometimes it felt like that world back there was even stranger than this one out here with the Faceless. At least out here I wasn't the only one who didn't fit in.

I thought again about how Doc had asked me what I wanted to be when we got home, and how I'd thought that I wouldn't mind mopping floors for a few years. But would I want to do that forever? Could I keep from snapping for the rest of my life? How far did Cam's patience with me go?

I'd ruin everything in the end, probably. I usually did.

"I think," I began, hating the tremulous tone in my voice, "that when we get home I need to talk to someone."

Cam threw me a questioning look.

"A shrink," I said. "I mean, they're mostly assholes too, but maybe not all of them are. I'm tired of hating everything, Cam. I'm tired of being angry all the time."

My voice broke on that, and Cam set his notebook down and climbed onto my bunk with me. He propped himself up on one elbow and curled his free hand around the back of my neck.

"Hey," he whispered, and I blinked away my sudden stinging tears. "Nothing you do, nothing you are, can ever make me stop loving you, okay?"

I nodded, my throat tight.

"You were right about me," he said. "I was so scared out here the first time, and there's like this room in my head where I've locked that part of me away, and sometimes I think he's still screaming, you know?" He swallowed, his throat bobbing. "Some-times I think that if I open that door, I won't be able to ever shut him up again, and that terrifies me like nothing else. You don't..." He swallowed again. "You don't have something like that in you. You don't have any locked doors inside you, and that's not a bad thing. It doesn't make you weaker. You're not a burden, Brady, and I'm not the only one doing the heavy lifting here, you know? We're both fucked up."

"So fucked up," I whispered back to him.

He showed me a shaky smile "And we both help each other."

"You'd tell me, wouldn't you, if I wasn't helping you anymore?"

"Yeah." He squeezed the back of my neck. "I'd tell you. But it wouldn't mean I didn't love you."

I'd always thought of Cam as the guy who was always saving me. I'd never thought I was saving him as well, or that maybe we were so tangled up in each other that we were just drowning together and pulling each other down. Would someone else tell us, I wondered, if they saw that happening, or would we both just sink to the bottom of the black ocean, struggling the whole way?

Cam saw my fear. He always did.

"We're okay, Brady," he said. "You and me, we're okay. We make it work. We save each other, remember? We always do."

"Yeah," I said. I closed my eyes and held onto that thought, that faith that Cam had in us against the universe. "We always do."

I WOKE up with a growling stomach and padded off to the nearest alcove. Lucy might have taken to these things like a duck to water but I would never like it. The ship took care of my hunger but it didn't take care of that voice in the back of my head that told me I hadn't actually eaten. I was too human, and too stubborn. I needed food in my belly and sunlight on my skin. I needed my feet in the dirt, and all the wonders of the universe would never change that about me.

I stripped my clothes off and stepped into the alcove. I squeezed my eyes shut as the alcove closed behind me, and then the walls expanded, filled somehow to compress around me. It was wet and dark, and then the alcove began to fill with fluid. It didn't matter how many times I did this. I always felt that same shock, that same visceral moment of *no*, when I inhaled that first breath of liquid.

I coughed reflexively, and the fluid flowed into my lungs.

It was easier after that. It was like swimming at night, my head under the dark water, suspended in the blackness except with no burning pressure in my lungs telling me I had to break the surface and breathe.

The others could stay for hours in the alcoves, nutrients feeding into them, toxins leaching out, but I'd never been great just spending time alone in my head. Cam tried to get me to meditate once. Fucking disaster that was.

"Just breathe and center yourself, Brady."

"What the fuck does that even mean? This is bullshit."

I was not at one with the universe. Not then and sure as shit not now.

I stayed in the alcove until my hunger pangs had vanished, and then dug my fingers into the seam in the wall to release me. I coughed again at the switch between liquid and air, and then stepped back out of the alcove. I wiped the fluid off me with my shirt, and then pulled my underwear and pants back on. I slung my shirt over my shoulder to hang it up when I got back to our room. There was no way to do laundry here. No water, and sure as hell no soap. The fluid just dried on our skin and on our clothes, and fell away in flakes.

I thought about Doc and how he'd asked me about my ambition. I reckon my one ambition was to get back to Earth and have a decent fucking shower. Which probably wasn't what he'd meant at all.

The room was empty except for Andre and Lucy when I got back.

I hung my shirt over the end of my bunk. "Where is everyone?"

"Doc and Harry are in the medbay, I think," Andre said. "No idea where Chris and Cam are."

"Chris went to an alcove," Lucy announced, looking up from her drawing. "He was pissed off because you took the closest one."

I'd have a go at her about her language except she probably picked it up from me. "He should have got up earlier then."

Lucy grinned at me. "That's what Cam said."

And then the smile faded from her face.

I turned.

There was a Faceless in the doorway, looking in at us. And...

And I couldn't feel him. There was nothing come off him at all. No emotion, no curiosity, no static buzz or back-and-forth of anything between us.

This Faceless was a stranger.

Andre moved to stand beside me, in front of Lucy. His shoulder knocked against mine, and that simple contact brought me out in goose bumps.

And then another Faceless stepped into view.

Kai-Ren.

He made a low hissing sound that I recognized was supposed to sound soothing, and beckoned me forward.

I froze.

"Bray-dee."

Both a command and an encouragement.

I stepped toward him, my heart pounding.

The Faceless—the Stranger—made a questioning sound and reached out a gloved hand toward me. He slid his fingers down my torso. He prodded my stomach, seemingly fascinated by the softness of my skin and the way it bowed under the slight pressure he exerted. I stared up into his mask while his fingers slid down my abdomen, and my faint reflection stared back at me.

What had Cam called me? A kid with eyes as big as an owl's.

The Stranger made a curious noise and jabbed his finger into my stomach, pushing a grunt out of me. I twisted away, one hand reaching out reflexively to put some space between us.

He caught my wrist, and tugged me closer. Dragged my arm up so that he could see my fingers trembling right in front of his mask. My weak human hand, nothing but soft pink skin and blunt nails. The Stranger hummed and leaned in, and fear froze me.

There was no connection between us. No confused white noise that sometimes approached almost-understanding. There was nothing.

And then Kai-Ren made a sound, and the Stranger released my wrist.

I took a step back from him, dizzy with adrenaline, my heart beating fast like a rabbit trembling under the scrutiny of a wild dog.

Kai-Ren and the Stranger left.

"Brady," Andre rasped. "You okay?"

I rubbed my stomach where the Stranger had jabbed it. It felt like it would bruise. I nodded, because I couldn't bring myself to speak yet.

"What was that?" Lucy asked. "Why couldn't we hear him?"

"He wasn't one of ours," Andre told her. "He must've been from one of the other ships."

I turned back toward them.

"You okay?" Andre asked again. I could feel his tension, his anxiety, as clearly as I could feel my own.

"Yeah," I said. "Just... just fucking Human Exhibit Number One in Kai-Ren's petting zoo, I guess, right?"

Andre's mouth quirked into an approximation of a smile, but there was no amusement in it. Just worry. We were powerless here. We always had been, but that didn't make the reminders any easier to bear.

"What's a petting zoo?" Lucy whispered.

I dragged my trembling fingertips over her hair. I guessed that was someplace Cam and I had never got around to taking her. "It's a place you can go and pet all the animals. Like goats and sheep and wallabies and shit, I don't know. When we get home, I'll take you to one, okay?"

"Okay." Her voice was shaky.

Another promise I wasn't sure I could keep. Add it to the list.

But empty or not, my promises made her happy. By the time Cam got back Lucy was sitting on her bunk drawing lopsided sheep and the trembling in my hands had subsided.

FACELESS DIPLOMACY, if that's what it was, was as incomprehensible to us as anything and everything that had come before. The Stranger was on our ship and then he was gone again, and if his presence had meant anything at all, then of course we'd be the last to know.

"Maybe this wasn't an official visit," Harry suggested that night as we played poker with the damp stained cards. "Maybe they're friends."

The idea of a Faceless having a friend was so crazy it made me laugh.

Cam grinned, and dug his elbow into my ribs. "Well, maybe not a friend as we understand it."

"Sure," Andre drawled. "Right now he and Kai-Ren are kicking back, having some booze, and talking about their old school days."

Even Doc laughed at that.

"Maybe he's a relative," Harry suggested. "A brother, or an uncle, or a cousin."

Andre hummed. "But he's not in this hive."

"Maybe the hives split," I said. "If they get too big or something."

"Huh," Doc mused. "Where do you suppose the queens come from then?"

"Fucked if I know," Andre said.

Chris tossed his cards down. "All this speculation is pointless."

"Cap," Harry said, his eyebrows tugging together. "Speculation is all we've got. At least it stops us going stir crazy."

Chris snorted. "I'm not so sure of that."

A joke? Jesus. The isolation must've been getting to him too.

"Okay," I said. "Who wants to raise the stakes here?"

"To what?" Andre asked.

"So back on Defender Three, we'd play for cigarettes and booze," I said. "And when we ran out of those, we'd play for the shit we wanted when we got home. Like this one guy, Cesari, he'd always bet a whole tray of his nonna's cannoli. Like I didn't even know what cannoli was, but the way he talked about it, you'd pretty much bust a—" I shot a look at Lucy. "Your mouth'd water, I mean, when he talked about it."

"How the hell do you send a tray of cannoli to a Defender?" Andre asked, raising his eyebrows.

"You don't," I said, taking the cards back and shuffling them. "None of us were ever going to taste that cannoli. That's not the point. The point is it stopped us from bouncing off the walls." I considered that. "Some of the time."

"I get it," Harry said. "Okay, so I'm going to bet my grandmother's scones. Jesus. You could turn up at her place any time of day, and half an hour later you'd be eating buttermilk scones straight from the oven. You'd burn your fingers pulling them open, they were so fresh, and she always had raspberry jam and clotted cream to go them with."

My stomach growled.

"How is that not torture?" Doc grizzled.

"What about you, Doc?" I asked.

"Fine. When I was in med school, there was this Thai place down the street from where I was living," Doc said. "Every Friday I used to go and buy ginger chili chicken with coconut rice. It'd blow your skull off it was so strong. I used to drink a whole quart of milk every time I ate it. It was a goddamn religious experience."

"Grandma's scones and ginger chili chicken," I said. "What've you got, Andre?"

"Poutine," Andre said with a grin.

Harry made a face.

"Nah." Andre punched him in the shoulder. "Don't give me that, man. Poutine is incredible. Fucking *scones*? Poutine is where it's at. With so much gravy you gotta eat it with a spoon."

Harry made another face just like the first one. "What about you, Chris?"

Chris exhaled heavily, and considered for a moment. "Calamari. Just salt and pepper calamari, cooked exactly right. Not stringy or rubbery. Just right." He shot a narrow glare at me. "This is messed up, Brady. Now I just want real food for once."

"No, it's good," I said. "You just gotta get into it."

I glanced at Cam, and saw him smiling at me, like I was doing something right. Something more than making us all hungry, at least.

"I like fairy bread," Lucy contributed. "We had some at my birthday party. It was yummy."

Then she had to explain fairy bread to everyone except me and Cam.

"Beach hot dogs," Cam said when it was his turn. "There's a food cart at the beach near our place back home, and honestly the hot dogs are pretty crap, but when you've been swimming for an hour, you know how starving you get? There is nothing better than a beach hot dog on a Saturday afternoon."

"What about you, Brady?" Andre asked, raising his eyebrows.

"I've got your number," I told him with a lazy grin. "You reckon some reffo from Kopa has got nothing on you lot, right? I'll bet every single one of you has eaten in some real fancy restaurants, and paid a shitload of money for some salmon or some bullshit oily fish like that. But have you ever tried barramundi? Freshly caught, and wrapped in foil and cooked on coals from the fire. Just a little bit of bush lemon, and you're set. And you sit around the fire, your toes in the sand, and you eat until it feels like your stomach will burst."

I closed my eyes and inhaled. Could almost smell the salt air. And that was the real trick of this game. Not to feel hungry, or to bitch about what we couldn't have. It was to get past that, just for a few minutes in our shitty unchanging days, and feel closer to home. Just for a little while.

Back on Defender Three it had let us escape the monotony, the drudgery, and the fact our days were full of intractable rules and even more intractable asshole officers. And here, on the Faceless ship, it let us forget for a moment that we were farther away from home than any humans had ever been before, and that we were entirely on our own, and that Kai-Ren and the Faceless were still—and would always be—unknowable to us.

We had each other, at least, for whatever that was worth, and talking about food lead inevitably to talking about family, and about friends. And it didn't matter that we'd been in each other's heads, because a story told is never quite the same as a story remembered. There's something in the telling of it that's bigger than the memory even if you've heard it a hundred times before. It's familiar and communal at the same time.

And maybe these guys were officers, and maybe back on their Defenders they'd had come at sharing their stories in a more civilized way—coffee and cigars, probably—but what did it matter as long as we got there in the end?

So we played cards and talked, and talked some more, and it almost felt like we were home.

And I had definitely done something right, because later that night Cam dragged me outside and up into that secret place that we called ours, and got down on his knees and blew me.

And after that he kissed me, and told me that he loved me, and the universe shrunk to just the two of us.

CHAPTER 7

BACK WHEN I was a kid in Kopa, there was a man who lived across the road who had lines in his leathery face as deep as ravines. Those lines caught all the shadows and held them. The ones on his cheeks and neck sprouted bristles his razor couldn't touch. He was old, with more years behind him than most people in Kopa got to see. His fingers were bent and twisted, with swollen knuckles, and his legs were as skinny as twigs. His eyes were watery slits. And every morning he'd stand outside the shack he lived in, lift his nose to the air and sniff it, and then tell us what weather was coming that day. He was never wrong. Dad said it was because he was so old he'd seen it all before, but I liked to imagine it was because he was magic. Whichever it was, we could have used someone like him on the Faceless ship, sniffing out the oncoming storm before it was even a shadow on the horizon.

Our ship slid through the nebula, and other ships glided along beside her. Sometimes they were nothing but shadows in the color-burst clouds, but sometimes they were close enough to block our views of anything beyond them. And sometimes they touched, melded, and opened their walls so that the Faceless could pass through them. Times like those were accompanied by low static in our connection—the faint buzz of interference from an overlapping network that remained encrypted to us.

The Faceless weren't socializing, not exactly, or at least not in any way that was recognizable to us. The nearest I could figure was that they were here to pay their respects to Kai-Ren, and to be shown all the markers of his strength: his ship, his hive, his pool of developing eggs, and his humans. Kai-Ren was like a king showing off his riches to his vassals, or maybe like that one asshole at the gym who flexes his muscles whenever someone looks at him. Fuck if I knew which one it was, or if there was even a difference. It was all dick measuring, right?

When other Faceless were aboard we stayed close to our room. Even Chris stayed away from whichever Faceless ship was connected to ours like a conjoined twin, because what if they separated again and he was on the wrong one? The thought of being alone out here, truly alone, must have been terrifying even to him.

Still, we got used to strange Faceless being on our ship sometimes. Got used to not feeling that flicker of recognition we got from those who shared our connection. Got used to their stares following us when they saw us.

Harry, less interested in Faceless tech than he was in the Faceless themselves, took copious amounts of notes on the way they interacted, his forehead creased as he wrote, coming up again and again against that same wall: how the fuck could we even begin to describe the Faceless when first we had to filter them through the narrow constraints of both our understanding and our language itself? It was hopeless, probably, but it didn't stop him from trying.

Fucking pointless.

I said as much to him one morning as we were both heading down to one of the alcoves. My belly was growling and as much as my brain told me it wasn't real food, I needed something.

"It's not *pointless*," he said.

I'd seen his notebooks. Pages and pages covered in weird marks that were his Faceless alphabet. Every different mark corresponding to one of the hissing sounds the Faceless made. And that was just cataloguing them, not even translating them, because where the fuck would he even start on that?

"I've seen your chicken-scratch bullshit," I said. "It's pointless."

He elbowed me. "But there's something there, you know? There has to be. Why would a race that can communicate telepathically also have a verbal language? It has to exist to fill a role that telepathy can't, right? So maybe if we can figure that out, we can actually learn to speak it."

"Or maybe they're totally alien and it's dumb to even try."

"Aren't you even curious though?" he asked, and there was something in his tone of voice, echoed in our connection, that made me think he felt sorry for me. For my short-sightedness. For my lack of imagination. For whatever deficiency it was he saw in me.

"No." My stomach ached, and it wasn't just from hunger. "I just want to go home and pretend none of this ever happened."

Of all of them, maybe it was Harry I should have had most in common with. He was only a couple of years older than me. We were the kids of the team, apart from Lucy, the literal kid. But there were whole universes between guys like me and guys like Harry. I'd seen his memories, and they were nothing like mine.

"Yeah?" he said, and elbowed me again. "Too bad, Brady, because when we get home, I'm gonna visit you and Lucy so often you'll get sick of the sight of my face."

"Too late," I said. "I already am."

His laughter carried us around the curve of the corridor, and right into the path of a Faceless.

A stranger.

Maybe *the* Stranger; the one that had touched me while Kai-Ren looked on.

He stared at us through his black mask, and made a humming sound, and a shiver ran down my spine.

It was the Stranger. The one that Kai-Ren had showed around the ship. The one he'd showed *us* to, like we were toys or trophies or trinkets, or some weird combination of all three, or something entirely different.

It was the not knowing—the never knowing *anything*—that made everything here so hard. It was like living in total darkness, blindly feeling our way with every step we took.

The Stranger stepped forward, tilting his head on an angle. Zeroed in on Harry like a dog on a scent. Made that humming sound again, and then reached out and curled his gloved fingers around Harry's throat.

My fear spiked.

"It's okay," Harry said, his gaze fixed on the Stranger. "It's okay, he's not hurting me."

The Stranger hummed again, a slightly higher pitch this time, almost as though he was asking a question. And maybe he was, but Harry and I were just stumbling around in the dark, weren't we? All the fucking time.

The Stranger leaned in close to Harry and Harry's fear spiked through him. I was standing close enough to feel the aftershocks of it in my gut.

I wondered what The Stranger was seeing. A pale-skinned human, face shaded with reddish stubble since he hadn't shaved in a day or two. A smatter of freckles over the bridge of his nose that even months in the black couldn't wash away, and red hair that had once been a sharp officer's haircut but was now mostly untamed scruff. Did Harry look any different to me to the Stranger's gaze, or did all humans look alike to them the way the Faceless did to us?

The Stranger hummed again, and loosened his grip on Harry's throat.

"I'm okay," Harry said again. He stared up at the Stranger and took a step back from him. He held out his palm as though that would stop him from following if he wanted. "It's just...it's just a form of communication we don't understand yet, right?"

Which one of us was he trying to convince?

He glanced at me quickly. "Let's use another alcove, yeah?"

"Yeah."

We backed up the way we'd come, leaving the Stranger staring after us and unease rising in our guts.

———————

HARRY HAD REDISCOVERED his enthusiasm by the time we reached the alcove on the level above our room.

"Like last night," he said, "when you got us all talking about food, you know what I was thinking?"

I shrugged.

"Food," Harry said. "It's such a universal thing to us, isn't it? All societies, all cultures, we all break bread. Food and stories. That's how we communicate. That's how we bond. Eating and talking is both communication and communion. So I figured the Faceless would have something like that, you know? That there'd be these shared activities like that, where we could watch them in action, and figure them out." He gestured to the alcove. "But they don't eat together, or sleep together. They go into separate places to do those things. And even when they're working together for a common purpose, like on this ship, they don't connect, you know? You know the shit they put you through in the military? Strap on your pack and run up that fucking hill? You hate it, but you're all in it together, right? You *bond*."

"If you say so," I said. "Your intake must've been different from mine."

Harry snorted. "Yeah, you're the outlier here, Brady, like always."

But he knocked our shoulders together when he said it.

"My point is, the Faceless don't seem to bond," he said. "It's like they don't need it like we do."

"That's a mammalian thing, isn't it?" I asked. "Ants don't bond. Sharks don't. Lizards don't."

"Don't they?" Harry wrinkled his nose.

"Yeah, fuck if I know." I nodded at the alcove. "Want to share?"

Harry laughed. "See? Even when we're not breaking bread, we're sharing a meal. That's very human of you, Brady."

"Apparently," I said, and we stepped into the alcove together.

I closed my eyes and the wall oozed shut behind us, and fluid began to fill the alcove.

That would never not be gross.

"YOU SON OF A BITCH," I told Doc as I rounded the doorway to his medbay and hour or two later. "You've been holding out on me."

Doc grinned and puffed on his cigarette. "Found this at the bottom of my footlocker."

I sat down beside him on the cot, and he passed the cigarette over to me.

Breaking bread, I thought, my eyes sliding shut as I took a long drag.

Shit, that was good. The taste, the heat. It had been so long since I'd had nicotine that I got a head rush out of it and everything, and Doc laughed at me. His hands were shaking too though when he took the cigarette back.

We passed the cigarette back and forth.

"Better than sex," I said, exhaling a stream of smoke into the humid air.

"You greedy little bastard, getting *both*." Doc took the cigarette back. "Keep rubbing it in my face, and I'll tell Rushton exactly how he compares to a cigarette."

Food and cigarettes and sex. I thought of what Harry had said earlier, and of the gulf between humanity and the Faceless. Sex sure as hell fascinated Kai-Ren. He'd watched Cam and me before. Watched us, and touched us, and drank in the emotions we shared when we were fucking. I thought of the eggs in the hatchery. I didn't know what they did to create those, but I couldn't imagine it involved anything like love. When Kai-Ren had raped Cam, had it even been sex to him? Or just some way to infect Cam with whatever virus or venom or what-the-hell-ever it was that had enabled them to communicate?

Did he even know what he'd done? Not then, but now? Now he'd seen us make love, did he *know*? There was no way to ask him that, probably. No way to make him understand the question.

Bile rose in the back of my throat.

Doc passed the cigarette back to me. "Where did you go just then, Brady?"

I took a drag on the cigarette and exhaled the smoky word: "Nowhere."

Doc side-eyed me.

"Just stir-crazy," I said. "Same old, same old. Just...I want to go home, Doc, and I'm scared shitless it'll never happen."

"Don't ever let that stop you fighting to make it happen."

I held the cigarette out and he waved it away. "Maybe that's the problem, Doc. There's nothing to fight against here, except time, and I can't fight your fucking clock, can I? Can't fight the Faceless. Can't fight the ship. The only thing I can fight here is you, or Cam, or the other guys, and I don't want to do that. We're in this together, right?"

"I think that's called personal growth, Brady."

"It sucks balls," I said. "And not in a fun way."

Doc huffed out a laugh, and slapped me on the back. "You got into plenty of fights on Defender Three. You weren't in it together with those guys?"

"There were hundreds of guys on Defender Three," I said. The cigarette tasted foul as the ember burned into the filter, and I stubbed it out on the metal edge of the cot regretfully. "There was no shortage of assholes there. I reckon I might be the only asshole onboard this ship."

"Oh, I don't know," Doc drawled. He scrubbed his hand over his shin, his whiskers rasping. "I'm pretty sure I can give you a run for your money, son."

Liar.

Doc was just about the greatest man I'd ever met. I wouldn't have survived on Defender Three without him, and he was here too, wasn't he? He was *here*, and that said more than any words ever could.

"Thanks, Doc." We sat in silence for a long while, and I rolled the cigarette butt between my thumb and forefinger, flattening it. "Can you believe that was our last one?"

Doc rolled his eyes. "Jesus, Brady. You can't just enjoy the moment, can you? If you've got a bruise, you've just got to keep poking it, don't you?"

"Sorry, Doc."

"No, you aren't, you little shit," Doc said. He shot me a narrow glare that I didn't believe for a second. "Someone once told you that misery loves company, and you've been making it your life mission ever since."

I grinned, unexpected delight bubbling up from some place inside me. I leaned closer to Doc to knock our shoulders together, and he scruffed a hand over my hair.

Moments like this, I almost thought we'd be okay. Moments like this, I almost thought we'd make it safely home and I'd feel the sunlight on my back again. Moments like this, I almost forgot how far out in the black we really were.

And moments like this were shattered as easily as glass.

A sudden burst of fear and panic lit up our connection like a lightning storm.

"The *fuck*?" Doc twisted around on the cot to stare at me.

"Wasn't me," I said, but my heart was pounding and the sudden dump of epinephrine into my system made me want to be sick. Bile rose in the back of my throat, sour and hot, and still that note of panic was ringing in the back of my skull as loud as a klaxon. "It's not me!"

Doc pushed himself up from the cot. "It's Harry," he said, striding out of the medbay. "It's *Harry*!"

I hurried out after him, my panic pushing me along more than anything. Maybe I was worried for Harry, for whatever was causing him to send that blast of fear through our connection, but I was selfish too. I didn't want to be left alone.

Doc barreled down the corridor. "Harry? *Harry*!"

The Faceless ship was strange and dark, illuminated by the glowing lights that bobbed along in the fluid in the walls. But they were as random as platelets in a bloodstream, sometimes floating along quickly—fireflies in our peripheral vision, there and gone again and leaving us stumbling in the dark—and sometimes stuck in bottlenecks of their own making, like a tangled string of Christmas lights that would light up a section of the ship for long minutes before they were swept away again.

Doc and I were a few turns of the spiral below the medbay when someone else came racing out of a side room: Chris.

"What's going on?"

"No fucking idea!" Doc sucked in a wheezing breath, and we kept going.

Harry's panic was louder now. It wasn't just in our heads anymore. I could hear him calling out. Or maybe he wasn't. Maybe he was just making noises. They weren't even words, really. They were short, choked off sounds of fear, of horror, of outrage and disbelief. They were a hundred different things, and none of them good.

My stomach churned.

I knew what those sounds meant. I'd made them before, back when I was a sixteen-year-old recruit on the filthy floor of a shower room on Defender Three. Made them on this exact ship too, except Cam had stopped Kai-Ren before he got as far as that asshole Wade back on Defender Three had.

Still, the memory was enough to bring me up short in the doorway of the room we found Harry in.

I froze, but Chris didn't.

"Hey!" he bellowed. "Hey! What the *fuck* are you doing?"

The Faceless didn't speak out language, but there was no hiding Chris's anger.

The Faceless standing over Harry—the Stranger—turned to face us. Tilted his head like a curious predator watching a bunch of fat, twitching mice and wondering which one to snap up first.

Chris barged forward into the room.

Another Faceless appeared beside me. Not Kai-Ren, but his

consciousness, that weird, static buzz, brushed against mine and it felt familiar. He was one of our hive then. The Faceless hissed and moved into the room.

Chris hauled Harry to his feet. His shirt was tattered and his pants were hanging around his thighs. Harry grabbed at them, missed, and stumbled as Chris tugged him toward the door.

"Okay," Doc said, reaching out to steady him as they reached us. "Let's go. Let's go."

Chris turned back as though he was ready to get back in there and face off with the Stranger. The Stranger and our Faceless were hissing and clicking like angry insects.

"Let's *go*," Doc growled.

"Chris!" I got on Harry's other side to help him.

Chris cast one more look back at the Stranger and our Faceless, then joined us hauling Harry up the corridor toward the medbay. Harry was still trying to hitch his pants up.

"You got him?" Chris asked. "You got him?"

"Yes!"

Chris peeled away from us.

"Where are you going?" I yelled after him.

He didn't answer.

He didn't have to.

I could hear him screaming the name in his mind as he bolted back down into the dark core of the ship: *Kai-Ren!*

Doc and I got Harry into the medbay. Gave him the chance to get his pants back up at last, then sat him down on the cot and tugged a blanket around his shoulders.

Doc crouched down in front of him, feeling for the pulse in his wrist. "Did he hurt you, Harry?"

Harry shook his head numbly. "No." His fingers curled around the edges of the blanket, tugging it closer in jerking increments. "He was going to, but..." He swallowed. "Just an attempt at form of communication we don't understand yet."

I glanced up to see Cam standing in the doorway.

"Just," Harry said. He stalled, and started again. "It's not—it's not—" He shook his head. "It's just we don't understand."

And then he sunk into silence, staring numbly at the lights floating in the walls.

I bet the Faceless ship, and the Faceless, has never seemed more alien to him than right now.

"NEW PROTOCOLS," Chris said quietly that night. "We try to limit our contact with the Faceless who aren't a part of Kai-Ren's hive. We don't leave this room unless we have to while they're on board. And if we do, we stay in pairs at all times. Agreed?"

Agreed? That was a question an officer in charge of a mission wouldn't have asked in any other place, but the rules were different here. The boundaries between us were different, and had been since the moment we'd starting living in each other's heads.

"The other Faceless are here to...*observe*," Chris said, his brows tugging together like the word didn't quite fit but was the best one he could come up with. "Kai-Ren says they're here to see the eggs. It's like a show of strength, or something, to have so many. It shows that Kai-Ren is powerful, that his hive is the strongest, the foremost, or something. So the other Faceless come to look, they're duly impressed, and then soon they'll go away again. We just have to keep out of their way until that happens."

Harry was curled up on his cot. He'd been quiet since his encounter with the Stranger, but we could all feel how he was struggling. And maybe nothing had happened in the end, and maybe it could have been a hell of a lot worse, but what consolation was that? Fucking none, because he'd had it shoved in his face exactly how powerless he was, how small he was, and how his agency, his wishes, his entire *self*, had meant nothing to the Stranger.

Cam had been there before.

So had I.

It was the sort of feeling it was impossible to ever forget.

Lucy was watching from her cot. She was quiet too. She

looked younger than she had that morning. We couldn't protect her from our fear. Couldn't hide it from her when she could feel it too.

Andre wiped a hand over his face. "What did Kai-Ren say about Harry?"

"What does Kai-Ren ever say?" Chris asked. "He was annoyed." His mouth twisted as though he was fighting a bitter smile. "Like a kid who finds out someone else touched his stuff."

Yeah, that sounded about right. The gulf between us and the Faceless? Unbridgeable from both sides.

I turned my head as I saw a flash of movement in the corner of my eye: Cam was striding out of the room.

"What did I just say?" Chris asked. "Cam!"

"I'll go!" I hurried after him.

I followed him up the incline of the corridor, past the alcove Harry and I had used that afternoon, and up into that strange, secret corner that felt almost like the hidden space under the roots of a banyan tree. Cam ducked underneath the twisting limbs that served some purpose we couldn't begin to guess at, and I followed him through.

Cam sat on the damp floor, his back to me, and drew his knees up.

I sat down behind him. Rubbed a hand down his back, and then rested my forehead on his shoulder. A tremor ran through him.

"I thought it didn't matter, what I felt," he said at last, his voice so soft it was almost lost to me, almost swallowed up whole by the darkness. "I thought that I could put it aside. Rationalize it. Reframe it so that it wasn't..."

I rubbed his back as another tremor went through him.

"So that it wasn't what it was," he whispered. "It was supposed to be different this time, Brady. He was supposed to understand."

Unbridgeable.

Cam straightened up, and I leaned back and slid my arms

around him. I splayed my fingers over his heart, as though I could hold that too. Hold it, and stop it from ever breaking.

Too late for that though.

Cam let out a shaky breath. "You're not the only one who wants to go home, Brady."

I closed my eyes and held him, and dreamed of sunlight.

CHAPTER 8

THE NEXT TIME the fear came, and the anger with it, it wasn't mine.

It was a night or two after the Stranger had tried to hurt Harry, if things like nights could even be counted in the black. We were asleep anyway, while the ship carried us further into the clouds of the nebula, and farther away from home than we'd ever been before. I don't know what I was dreaming of—red dirt, probably, and the sun on my back—but I came up gasping for air and I wasn't the only one.

"The fuck?" Andre was already climbing down from his bunk. "What... what was *that*? What is that?"

It was like ice in my blood. Like my nerve endings were being drawn out like wires, pulled and twisted. There was a high-pitched whine in the back of my skull, like a screech of radio feedback. It was cold fear, and it was burning anger, and it was meeting in the middle in a discordant howling maelstrom, and for once it wasn't coming from me.

It was coming from the Faceless.

My first instinct was to run. Something bad enough to scare the Faceless? You can bet I wanted to be nowhere fucking near it. The moment the frantic urge caught me, I almost laughed at the absurdity of it. Because where the hell could I go? Where could any of us go?

"Brady?" Lucy leaned over the edge of her bunk, her complexion pallid and consumptive in the blue lights of the nebula. "What's happening?"

I climbed out of my bunk and reached for her. "I don't know." I looked to Cam just like Lucy looked to me. "I don't know."

"What do we do?" Harry asked, swinging down from the bunk above Cam's. He clenched and unclenched his fists at his sides. "What do we do?"

Another soundless wave of fear and anger crashed over us, and Lucy whimpered and clung closer to me.

"Is that..." Doc shook his head as though to clear it. "Is that coming from *inside* the ship?"

I looked to Cam again, my throat suddenly dry and my heart racing.

And Cam looked to Chris.

And then Chris was moving, striding out of our room and into the core of the ship. He was fucking fearless, I'll give him that.

I peeled Lucy off me and into Harry's arms.

"Wait here," I said. "Wait here with her."

Because I knew Cam was going to follow him. And I knew I was going to follow Cam. Some things were written in the stars, however fucking dumb they were.

I caught up with Cam outside our room, and we descended the spiraling corridor together. The air around us seemed to pulse and spike, and my skin prickled with it. The closer we got to the core of the ship the louder the blast of fear and rage was in the back of our skulls. It jarred my bones and set every nerve on edge and sat queasy and heavy in my gut like something rancid.

We didn't see the Faceless as we wound our way deeper into the heart of the ship. Not a single one.

We found Chris standing in front of a wall, his shaking hand pressing against it. He turned when we approached him, his face lit up with the glow of the things that slid through the walls like jellyfish.

"I think it's coming from here," he said.

"That's the hatchery," Cam said. "That's where Kai-Ren showed us the eggs."

Chris swallowed, and closed his eyes, and then pushed through the wall.

And Cam and I followed.

When I blinked my eyes open again, slick fluid clinging to my eyelashes and sticking to my mouth, we were standing in the large, vaulted chamber with the shallow pool inside. Except it wasn't quiet this time. It was...

It was full of Faceless. The Faceless, and *things*. Pale, naked things that twitched and writhed on the floor, the skins of their sacs ripped open. They were like twisted, deformed specimens from jars of formaldehyde, and the Faceless were walking amongst them, snapping their necks.

Their rage was a solid wall of noise in my head now, pushing me back.

Kai-Ren was in the middle of it. He was standing in the pool and dragging his gloved hands through the steaming fluid like he was trawling for bait. He hauled a sac out of the pool. If it had been a tiny egg containing nothing but a flickering heartbeat a few days ago, it was easily as big as a human now. It was shorter than an adult Faceless. Kai-Ren flung the sac out of the pool onto the floor, and then stepped out after it.

The surface of the sac writhed and ululated, and Kai-Ren leaned down and tore it open. The pale, naked thing inside slithered free, and I remembered the first time I'd ever seen Cam, bursting out of that Faceless pod on Defender Three in a wave of stinking amniotic fluid.

Kai-Ren lifted the thing by the throat.

"No!" Chris yelled, darting forward through the killing grounds towards him. "No! Stop!"

Kai-Ren lifted his blank, masked face to stare at him.

"No!" Chris said again. He was a full head shorter than Kai-Ren, but he stood his ground. "Don't!"

Kai-Ren tilted his head, and let the twitching thing drop to the floor.

"What are you doing?" Chris asked him. "Why are you killing them? They're her children, aren't they? Her young?"

Kai-Ren didn't speak. He hissed, like steam escaping, and projected the word directly into our minds: "*Abomination.*"

"What do you..." Chris trailed off as he looked down at the thing. "Oh God." He twisted back to look at us. "It's not Faceless. It's... it's part *human.*"

My blood ran cold.

"Let me have it," Chris said. "Please. Let me have it."

Kai-Ren stared at him. "Why?"

"Because I want it," Chris said, like that was all that counted, and maybe that was the only answer that a cold thing like Kai-Ren could understand. He'd taken Cam that day in the black because he'd wanted, hadn't he? And that was all the reason he'd needed.

Chris stood in the middle of the hatchery, stubborn and fearless, and audacious enough to make a demand of Kai-Ren. The expression on his face was the sort they put on statues of heroes and generals. It was hard and unyielding and totally unafraid. But what the hell did that matter to Kai-Ren when he could swat Chris like an insect? Courage was such a human thing, and here, in Kai-Ren's hatchery, it was totally meaningless.

Except then Chris began to speak.

"Abomination?" he asked.

Kai-Ren hissed.

"It's waste," Chris said. "It's trash. It's of no value to you, so let me have it."

A whisper passed through the gathered Faceless like a breath of wind through dry eucalypts, hissing and rustling back and forth along our shared connection. If there were words in it, we couldn't hear them, but Kai-Ren tilted his head as though to listen.

"Take it then," Kai-Ren said. "Kill it when it is of no more interest to you."

"Thank you," Chris said, his eyes wide. "Thank you."

Cam stepped forward through the twitching bodies of the dying young to help him carry the sole survivor out.

THE FACELESS—THE hybrid, Chris called it—was as white as alabaster the way the Faceless were, but it didn't take more than a cursory inspection in the medbay to see that it was very different from them. It had a nose, for starters, instead of slits in its face like a reptile. It had eyelashes too, as dark as the patchy fuzz on its head. Its eyes were closed, its heartbeat weak. There was hardly any rise and fall to its chest at all.

"Jesus Christ," Doc said as he leaned over the thing. "Look at this, Brady."

He tilted the hybrid's chin back.

"Shit," I said. "It's got a proper larynx."

Doc levered its mouth open. "A tongue as well. Jesus. It might actually be able to talk."

Chris, leaning in the doorway of Doc's makeshift medbay, stood up straighter at that, his eyes bright as a million sudden potential scenarios floated in front of him. Scenarios where he could *talk* to a Faceless. He clenched and unclenched his fists at his sides as though he was fighting the urge to push between me and Doc and immediately start discussing eighteenth-century literature with the hybrid or some shit like that.

"Don't count your chickens, Varro," Doc said. "It might not even survive. Fuck knows how much longer it should have had before it hatched. It might not have any higher brain function. It might be so premature its lungs haven't developed properly yet." He paused for a moment. "If it even has fucking lungs."

Chris shifted from foot to foot, his brows pulling together.

At the back of my mind I could still feel Kai-Ren's rage and fear. It had faded, but what if he blamed us for this? The Faceless ship had come here so it could breed, and we'd fucked that up for it somehow.

Doc and I had a few theories on that as well.

The ship—the queen—reproduced asexually. She probably used the genetic material that was floating around in her, like a template or whatever. And we'd been infesting her like ticks for the past few months, feeding and sleeping inside her, and excreting saliva and sweat and blood and waste and —in Cam's and my case, at least—cum into her. We'd poisoned the well with our human DNA and we'd destroyed an entire breeding cycle.

There was a very good chance that Kai-Ren was going to kill us for this. We'd caused the queen to produce abominations.

Doc laid the end of his stethoscope on the hybrid's chest.

I looked at the hybrid's hands instead of its face. I'd rarely seen Kai-Ren without his mask, let alone his gloves. The Faceless didn't wear clothing, but a protective layer of synthetic goo that the ship provided that was as thin as latex and as impenetrable as steel. Whatever it actually was it was easier to call them gloves, just like it was easier to call parts of the ship walls and floors and windows. We had to fit everything into our human frames of reference, and sometimes that meant forcing ourselves to forget that everything here was literally alien. The hybrid had four fingers on each hand, and opposable thumbs. Its fingernails were more claw-like than a human's, but didn't appear retractable like the claws of the Faceless.

Its white skin wasn't as hard like the skin of the Faceless, but not as elastic as a human's either. It was cold to the touch, like theirs.

It had a dick too. External genitalia would be the technical term I guess, like a human male's, with thin patches of dark hair around it that looked stark against that bone-white Faceless skin.

I couldn't decide if the fact it looked more human than a Faceless made it less horrifying to look at, or more.

Doc caught my gaze, and I knew he was wondering the same thing.

"Will he live?" Chris asked from the doorway.

"I have no idea," Doc said. "I can't even tell if he's actually dying, let alone treat him."

"That's weird though," I said.

"How is it weird?" Doc groused, his bushy eyebrows tugging together. "It's a fucking alien, son, and way out of my skill set." "Yeah," I said. "But we all live in each other's heads now, and we can feel the Faceless too. This one's not linked in though, is it?" "Mmm." Doc watched the rise and fall of the hybrid's chest for a moment. He glanced at Chris, and I felt his unease prickling the back of my mind. "How many of them did you say Kai-Ren killed?"

I forced down my nausea at the memory of those broken twitching things on the floor of the hatchery. "The rest of them. Maybe a dozen?"

"Then whatever you're thinking," Doc said, and I realized he was talking to Chris now, and not to me, "don't do it."

"You don't know what I'm thinking," Chris said quietly.

"I can read you like a book, Varro," Doc shot back. "You want to communicate with this thing, you figure out some other way to do it. If Kai-Ren wants it dead, I somehow doubt he's going to want it hooked up to our connection."

A jolt of fear thrilled through me, and I stared at Chris.

Chris shrugged. "I thought about it. Doesn't mean I don't know it's not worth the risk. I felt his anger too. I wouldn't make a target of us." He fixed his gaze on mine. "Not any of us."

Lucy, I thought. *He means Lucy.* Because however much I didn't like Chris Varro and he didn't like me, he shared my memories of Lucy, of holding her when she was small, and wearing her in a sling against my skinny chest. Of her heartbeat thrumming against mine.

Chris Varro didn't like me much, but he felt the things that I felt and he couldn't escape that. He might drag the rest of us through fire to learn about the Faceless, but he wouldn't do it to Lucy. He wouldn't risk her, because even if his love for her was only an echo of mine it resonated in him. It was real.

I looked back to the hybrid for a moment, and then met Doc's gaze.

"Varro," Doc said. "Give us some room to work, hmm? I'll let you know the second anything changes."

Chris nodded, and peeled himself off the doorway and left.

Doc set his stethoscope down and sighed. "You okay, son?"

"Yeah." My throat clicked as I swallowed the lie.

Doc regarded me steadily for a moment. "You've seen it, haven't you? The resemblance."

I looked at the hybrid's dark hair. At the shape of its nose, its jaw. At the truth I'd been trying to deny since I realized how the hybrid had been made. My heart beat fast in my chest. "Yeah."

It was just dumb chance that this was the one Kai-Ren didn't kill. Just dumb chance that he got to the others first. There was nothing special about this one, except this one was mine. This one had been made from me. Looking at the hybrid was like looking in a funhouse mirror and seeing my reflection twisted up and made grotesque.

Doc held my gaze.

"Could have been any one of us," I said at last.

"It could have been," Doc agreed. "It's not though, is it? So I'll ask you again. Are you okay?"

I looked at the rise and fall of the hybrid's chest. "I wish he'd killed this one too."

"That's fair," Doc said. "I'd probably feel the same in your shoes."

"Anything in your philosophy books about this?"

Doc's face cracked with a rueful smile. "Oh, I reckon this is more than your run of the mill existential crisis, don't you?"

That pulled an unwilling grin out of me. "Yeah, probably."

"We'll figure it out," Doc said.

"I fucking doubt it." I swallowed. "We're contaminants, aren't we? We were interesting to him once, but we've poisoned the well. What's to stop Kai-Ren from ripping us all apart like he did to the rest of the hybrids?"

Doc looked grave. "His word?"

"What's that worth though?" I asked. "We're nothing to the Faceless, Doc. We're *insects*. We always have been."

"I don't know what it's worth, Brady. I wish I did." Doc stepped away from the cot. He rolled his shoulders and inhaled deeply. "Do you know what I thought when I decided to come with you?"

I shook my head.

"I'm an old man, son," Doc said. "I've got almost forty years on you. I've lived my life. My kids are all grown. And I looked at you, and I looked at Lucy, and I wondered what sort of man I'd be if I let both of you go out into the black on your own. What sort of man I'd be if I let a scared kid do that, knowing there was a good chance they might not come back."

My throat ached and my chest was tight. "Lucy was never scared."

Doc smiled again. "I wasn't talking about Lucy, son."

I blinked, and my eyes filled with tears.

"Come here," Doc said.

I felt like a little kid as I stepped into his embrace and his arms went around me.

"I love you, son," Doc said, and I squeezed my burning eyes shut. "Just so we're clear, you were never just another recruit to me. I hope you know that."

I nodded. "I know."

Doc rubbed my back. "And I'm proud of you, Brady, for what it's worth—"

"Everything," I mumbled. "It's worth everything."

"I'm proud of you," Doc repeated, his voice rasping a little. "And your dad would be proud of you too."

I dug my fingers into the back of his shirt. I didn't ever want to let go.

"Whatever happens here is out of our control," Doc said. "And I don't know how this is going to end, Brady, but you're not alone. Whatever happens, I've got your back. I've got your back for as long as I can."

"Me too," I mumbled in his shirt. "I've got yours too. For whatever it's worth."

Doc's chest rumbled with a gentle laugh as he patted my back. "Everything, son. It's worth everything."

I leaned back at last, and looked him in the eye. His were as wet as mine. "We've got this, Doc."

"Yeah," he agreed, and it didn't matter if it was bullshit. "We've got this."

———————

I DIDN'T WANT to go back to the hatchery, back into the hidden core of the ship, but I could feel that's where Cam was. I kept my eyes closed as I passed through the wall and into the warm, viscous fluid that flowed around me. I held my breath, and my lungs burned by the time I pushed through into the hatchery and the walls oozed shut behind me.

Kai-Ren stood by the steaming pool. Cam stood in front of him, his chin tilted up. Kai-Ren held him in place with a finger under his jaw. The tension in the hatchery was thick, but I couldn't read any anger coming off Kai-Ren, or any fear from Cam. This display of dominance though, if that's even what it was...I wondered if this was Cam paying some price for Chris's earlier rebelliousness.

Kai-Ren saw me and dropped his gloved hand, and Cam turned his head to watch me approach. His face was drawn, his expression grave.

I couldn't look at the bodies on the floor. I was too afraid I'd see a face I knew. I only glanced down once, to pick a path over to the pool without stepping on them. The floor was sticky and wet underneath my bare feet, and my stomach roiled even as I tried to tell myself that this was no different than any other room in the Faceless ship. It wasn't blood. It was just the amniotic fluid that had surrounded the hybrids in their sacs. It was probably the same stuff from the pods, or from between the walls. It wasn't a horror movie if I didn't look.

I kept my gaze fixed on Cam as I closed the distance between us.

"Brady," he murmured, and held out a hand for me.

Most times when we stood together in front of Kai-Ren, I

curled into Cam. Not today. Today I faced him—god, demon, savior, scourge—and stared at his black featureless mask. There was no part of me that was hidden to Kai-Ren, no corner of my brain he hadn't seen into, and yet he was still utterly unknowable to me.

Chris thought we could understand the Faceless one day. Even Cam thought it. But here we stood in a room full of the bodies of the living things he'd killed, and Kai-Ren was as cold-blooded as always.

"You don't have children," Cam said, his voice quiet. "These were hive mates, not children. Do you feel anything for them?"

Kai-Ren gave a low hiss, and the word echoed in our minds: "Abominations."

"Do you blame us for that?" Cam asked him.

Another low, disgruntled hiss.

"We didn't know," Cam said. "When you brought us aboard, we didn't know this could happen. You didn't know, so how could we?"

Cam had been humanity's advocate before, alone in the black when those who loved him had already mourned him. He'd been fighting for humanity when we'd all thought he was a dead man. He'd been alone the first time he'd argued that we deserved to live. He wasn't alone now.

His fingers tightened around mine. "We didn't know. This isn't our fault, master." His voice hitched on that word he hadn't used in months, and I wondered if it was a title Kai-Ren had given himself, or one that Cam had fashioned, like battle regent, to make sense of the Faceless. To attempt to shape order out of chaos. "You swore a treaty. You said there would be peace. You promised you'd take us home again. Tell me that nothing has changed, please."

Kai-Ren stared down at him.

"Master," Cam repeated, and tugged his hand free from mine. He raised it, resting his fingers on Kai-Ren's shoulder for a moment before he stepped closer and curled his hand around the back of Kai-Ren's neck.

The mask fell away, and Kai-Ren's white, corpse-like face

turned toward mine. His eyes were yellow.

I wondered if he looked at us and thought we were grotesque.

Did the Faceless have nightmares about humans?

"This wasn't our fault," Cam said. He pressed his hand to Kai-Ren's cold, sunken cheek. "Please, master."

Kai-Ren curled his fingers around Cam's wrist and held his hand there. Cam's name escaped him on a low wheezing rasp. "Cam-ren."

"Please."

The complicated sounds we made were impossible for him, so Kai-Ren sent the words down our connection: "I will take you back."

I hadn't known how tense I was, how frightened, until relief washed over me.

Home.

Kai-Ren would take us home.

Even the thought of a rust-bucket of a Defender sounded like fucking heaven right now. Stale ration packs and cold showers. The stink of hundreds of guys stuck in close quarters. Asshole officers everywhere. Fuck, I wanted it so bad. I'd hated every minute I'd spent on Defender Three as a conscripted recruit, but I'd give anything to be back there. Irony's a fucking bitch, right? But as long as the bitch was on my side in the end, I'd laugh right alongside her. I'd tried to be brave out here. I'd tried to put my fear aside. And maybe once or twice I'd even convinced myself I'd done it. But Jesus, I just wanted to go home.

Kai-Ren released Cam's wrist and hissed again. It was a low sound, and possibly it was meant to be comforting. There was no real way of knowing, and wasn't that what bit at Chris the most? That in three months aboard this ship, inside this Faceless queen, there was still no real way of knowing.

We'd go home as ignorant as we had been before.

I closed my eyes as Kai-Ren reached toward me and tried not to flinch away from his touch as his gloved fingers, slightly damp, ran down the side of my face.

But we'd go home.

CHAPTER 9

THE HYBRID DIDN'T DIE in the night like Doc thought it might. It breathed shallowly as the light from the nebula shone on the walls in swirls of blue and green. Its eyes were open in thin dark slits though it was impossible to tell if it was actually conscious or not. Doc took its pulse every hour, and listened to its heart, and nothing much seemed to change.

"You oughta go get some sleep," Doc said at one point.

I shook my head.

"Some food then."

"We're out of food."

Doc grunted. "You know what I meant."

Yeah, I knew, but I didn't want to step inside the alcoves again. Not until I had to. Not when the result of us relying on the ship to live was lying on a cot in front of me wearing a grotesque approximation of my face.

"What about it?" I asked. "How long until it starves to death?"

Doc shrugged. "I have no fucking idea, son."

But of course Chris had a possible solution for that. He turned up in the middle of the night with two tin cups full of fluid he'd taken from inside one of the alcoves. He painstakingly dribbled the contents of one cup into the hybrid's mouth, holding its head up so it didn't choke and massaging its throat until it bobbed and swallowed.

We had no idea if it would work, but Doc didn't object. It wasn't as though we had any other options. It was literally this or nothing. I would have voted for nothing if it had been my choice. But since when was it my choice?

After the hybrid drank, Chris took the other cup of fluid and rubbed it over the hybrid's skin.

"Is it even the same stuff from inside the sacs?" I asked.

"Stinks the same," Chris said, which was about as accurate as we could get, I guess.

His words were dismissive, but his touch, as his hands slid over the hybrid's body, was strangely gentle. I watched those hands, strong and square, sliding through the fluid and remembered all the times I'd dreamed about them before I'd even known him.

A flutter of memory that wasn't mine: a litter of kittens, blind and mewling, and a twelve-year-old kid who'd set his alarm to wake up every two hours to bottle feed them. Even then Chris hadn't backed down from a challenge. I don't think he knew how.

I watched him for a moment longer, then looked over at Doc. "I'm going to go to bed."

Doc nodded at me as I left.

I wasn't tired, but I went to our room anyway. I checked that Lucy was sleeping, and then lay down on my bunk. I stared at the way the canvas dipped under Lucy's weight above me, and remembered that time on Defender Three that I woke up to the sound of old canvas ripping, and suddenly O'Shea was landing right on top of me, all knees and elbows and hard skull thunking against mine. We'd both got cracked ribs out of that, and I'd been angry at O'Shea for weeks, even though it wasn't his fault. It was easier to be angry than to show I was hurt, I think, in case someone thought I was weak.

I'd hated Defender Three and every day I'd been stuck there breathing in that stale, recycled air, with nothing between me and the vacuum of space but a few flimsy walls. I'd never made friends

—not close ones, at least. There were guys I talked shit with, and drank with, and played cards with, but they wouldn't have cared if I'd fallen out an airlock, and vice versa. Doc had been the only guy who'd really looked out for me, and back then a part of me had hated it because I thought it was just pity.

Cam was the first person who ever made me feel that maybe I wasn't weak. That it was okay to feel things. That it was okay to be angry, and hurt, and sad, and frightened, and it didn't make me small. It didn't make me less. He saw past all that, because there hadn't been a single stray thought that crossed my mind that he couldn't hear. There hadn't been any walls between us, and it had been terrifying.

I wasn't that same guy now that I had been. Maybe. He was still there, and he was still scared and angry, but he had Cam, and Lucy, and Doc. He had Harry and Andre as well. He even had Chris Varro. He wasn't alone, and that counted for something. That counted for more than I'd known. I'd taken some big steps since the first moment I'd met Cameron Rushton. And maybe from the outside it looked like I'd hardly moved, but it was a question of scale. My universe was a very small one. Those steps still counted.

I closed my eyes for a moment, and I was back in Kopa. I was a kid, and I was watching Lucy take her first steps in the dusty front yard of our shitty house. I was leaning on the sagging wire fence, and the sun was blinding me, and Lucy stood up and staggered a few steps, and then fell back down on her ass again. Tiny, tiny steps, but suddenly she was in a whole new world.

The canvas above me creaked as Lucy rolled over in her sleep.

Jesus, if Dad could see us now! His dirty reffo kids, floating in a nebula a million miles from Kopa. But we were coming home now. We were coming home. We'd been further than any humans had ever been before, but we were coming home.

I watched the strange lights from the nebula playing on the wall, and then closed my eyes again and imagined what it would feel like to wake up again with the sunlight on my face.

IT WAS dark when I awoke.

The whirls of blue light that had last illuminated the room had been swallowed by blackness. I turned my face toward the window and saw that the clouds of the nebula had vanished. So had the stars. Only the faint shifting light of the strange pulsing things that moved between the walls of the Faceless ship remained.

There was someone standing by the window, although maybe it was only a trick my eyes were playing on me—pulling inky shapes out of the darkness and attributing form to them. There was a word for that, but I'd forgotten it. It was an instinct hard-wired into us by evolution, a rush of adrenaline when we stared into mottled leaves and thought we glimpsed a face staring back, or saw the shape of a predator in the shifting shadows. Humans had thought we were the top of the food chain once, but even now our biology reminded us of what we really were: prey.

I climbed out of my bunk, the canvas creaking, and shuffled over to the window.

There was a man standing there. Chris. He turned to look at me as I approached. He didn't say anything. He just stepped aside to make room for me at the window.

I looked out into the black, and that's all I saw.

It was as though the universe had blinked entirely out of existence and left absolutely nothing behind.

A fear deeper than any one I'd ever known took root in my gut.

"It's a ship," Chris said, and I knew he could sense my fear and that he needed to soothe it before it poisoned him as well. "It's another Faceless ship. It's drawn up alongside us, that's all."

I exhaled, and let my nascent fear go on that shaky breath.

Chris stared out the window again. "It was like watching an eclipse."

Of course he'd watched fearlessly as the dark ship had swallowed our light. I'd once thought Cam was chasing starlight, but

Chris seemed to be chasing something altogether more intangible than that. I wondered if there was anything in the universe that would ever satisfy him.

He smiled in the faint light, and nodded his head toward the door. "Come on."

I looked over at the bunks, but I couldn't sense anyone else awake.

I followed Chris out into the corridor and, unsurprisingly, down into Doc's medbay where the hybrid lay on a cot. Doc was sitting on one footlocker, his feet propped up on another. He was leaning against the wall, his head tilted back. He was snoring.

The medbay was as dark as our room had been.

I crossed over to Doc and shook him awake. "Go to bed, Doc."

He stretched, his old joints cracking. "What?"

"Go to bed," I said. "I've got this."

He hauled himself to his feet. "You sure?"

"Yeah. Hourly obs, and it'll probably die anyway."

"That's about the gist of it, yeah." Doc clapped me on the shoulder, and then squinted around the room. "Why the fuck is it so dark?"

"There's another ship blocking out the windows from this side," I told him.

"Hmm." Doc didn't ask if that was anything we should be worried about, because what the hell was the point of asking? Chris wouldn't be able to give him an answer, and I sure as shit didn't have a fucking clue. "Okay. Call me if his condition changes."

"Yeah," I said. "I know."

Doc had once said he liked me for my bedside manner, but what he'd really meant was that I could sit beside a guy with half his face burned off, a guy who was crying in pain as he died, and I didn't even flinch. Why would I? I wasn't the one dying.

I'd liked the medbay because sick rations were better than regular rations, and half those guys couldn't finish their meals anyway. The medbay had also meant access to drugs, which were worth a shitload on the station black market, but I only did that a few times. The trainee medic gig had been a good one and I hadn't wanted to fuck it up by getting caught.

Point is, I knew the drill when it came to sitting beside guys and taking their vitals so Doc could go deal with other stuff or catch some sleep. I knew when it was worth bothering him with some change or not. Doc had trusted me with that a long time before now. He trusted me with it to the ends of the universe, it turned out.

"Get some sleep," I told him. "It's your turn."

Doc squeezed my shoulder and left the medbay.

I sat down on his footlocker and picked up his notes. Checked the hybrid's vitals. They were stable, I guess, but whether they were good or not there was no way to tell.

Chris sat down on the other footlocker and stared at the hybrid in the gloom.

I set the notes aside, and didn't look at the hybrid. Fucking thing creeped the hell out of me. I stared at the floor instead, and tried to not let the silence get to me. I'd never liked silence. Silence gave me too much room to think, and that usually led me into some fucked-up headspace that was impossible to escape. It usually led me to blurting out some bullshit too, just to try to get a reaction. I'd once had a shrink ask if I'd ever been diagnosed with Oppositional Defiance Disorder. I was just allergic to assholes, I think, and the problem in the military is that you're surrounded by them, day in and day out. That shrink had been an asshole too. Most officers were.

I lifted my gaze and looked at Chris.

I wouldn't have been so conflicted once, but I couldn't hate Chris. Cam had loved him, and there was an echo of that feeling still there, or at least the realization that it had been true once. And he'd loved Cam too. So he was still an asshole, probably, but not a total asshole. And I'd seen inside his head too often to pretend he was easy to categorize.

"You're jealous of me," I said at last.

Chris snorted. "I had him first."

"I wasn't talking about Cam," I said. "I'm talking about everything else. I experienced the Faceless connection before you did. I met Kai-Ren before you did. No fucking way did I qualify for this mission, but here I am. Everything that you would have given your right hand for, I got thrown into and I didn't even fucking want it." I nodded at the hybrid. "And that's my DNA in that thing there. That's a new form of life that the universe has never seen before, and it exists because of me, not you. It's killing you, isn't it?"

Chris smiled and dipped his head to hide it.

"Fuck you. I'm right, and you know it."

"No." He shook his head. "I'm not jealous of you, Brady. I've seen inside your head." He looked up at me again, his smile gone. "I might be jealous of Cam though."

A sharp emotion I couldn't name sliced through me, as hot as sudden anger, and then it was gone again, leaving me unbalanced and unsure of the ground underneath my feet.

"We were good together," Chris said, his voice low. "We were both ambitious, both smart, both going places. We were perfect, on paper." He exhaled slowly. "But we couldn't make it work. I mean, neither of us cared enough to make it work, to compromise or to make changes, you know? And that was fine. That was okay. We were young, and I guess a part of me always figured we'd get a second chance at some point, but it's not like I'd lose sleep over it if we didn't. And then he met you and it all changed."

"No," I said, swallowing. "He met the Faceless."

"No," Chris said. "I've been in his head too, remember? It wasn't just the Faceless. He met you, Brady. The universe wasn't big enough for Cam back when I knew him, but then he met you and now all of that has changed. He's changed. He's found what he was looking for, Brady, and it turns out it was this unmitigated fucking disaster of a human being. No offence." His teasing smile was back briefly, and then gone again. "And for some reason you make him happy. So yeah, I think that maybe I'm jealous of Cam."

"I knew it," I said, my heart thumping. "You think I'm hot."

He laughed. "That's what you get from that?"

There was no anger in his words though. He knew I was full of bullshit. The whole fucking universe knew that.

"Just calling it how I see it," I said.

He laughed again. "Sure."

We fell into silence for a while, but it was more comfortable than before. I watched the hybrid's chest rising and falling in the gloom.

"So what is it you're looking for, Chris?" I asked him at last.

He shrugged, and held my gaze. "I don't know. I just hope I'll know it when I see it, like Cam did."

And maybe, for the first time since I'd known him, I discovered that I didn't hate Chris Varro even a little bit, and I hoped he'd find whatever he was looking for too.

"Are you pissed we're going home?"

Chris shrugged again. "Maybe. It's the safest thing, I know that, but we won't get an opportunity like this one again. How can we, if just being on this ship does...*that?*" He gestured at the hybrid. "I wish we'd had more time here. I feel like we've hardly been given a glimpse of the Faceless, and now even that's being taken away from us."

"How did you...how were you never scared of them?" I was half afraid to ask the question. It revealed more about me than it did about anything, but I also wanted to know.

Chris's mouth quirked. "I'm terrified of them, Brady."

"You're not."

"I am." He dragged his fingers through his hair, leaving it mussed up. "You always say we're insects to the Faceless, right? And you're right. The thing is though, we're insects whether we're up here buzzing in their faces, or living in the ants' nests we call cities back on Earth. We're not safer when we're at home. We just lie to ourselves and say that we are so that we can actually function enough to live our lives. The Defenders are useless. Anyone who's ever been on one knows that. I'm as scared of the Faceless as anyone. I just figured it didn't make a difference *where* I was scared of them, so I might as well be standing right in front of them."

"Jesus." I snorted. "You and I have very different fear responses."

"Same fear though," he offered.

Yeah. Same fear. The difference was that Chris didn't let his fear cripple him. And whatever he said, however much he tried to downplay that, it was a hell of a difference.

"And what about the hybrid?" I asked.

Chris looked over at it. "I want to take him home," he said. "If Kai-Ren lets me. And if he survives."

Delivering a Faceless hybrid to the military would make up for our failures to deliver anything else useful, probably. Not that I gave a fuck if the military thought we'd failed—and Chris probably didn't either. That's not how he measured failure and success. But the hybrid also represented knowledge, and Chris burned for that.

I watched as the hybrid's pale fingers twitched against the cot. "You think Kai-Ren will let you take it?"

"I think Kai-Ren doesn't give a shit what happens to him," Chris said, and shrugged. "Unless he thinks we could somehow use him against the Faceless."

"I don't think he thinks we're smart enough for that."

Chris shrugged. "And he's probably right."

"Does it matter that it's a—"

A living thing? A thing that could feel pain, maybe? Possibly even a sentient thing? What would scientists do to it back on Earth? And what would it mean if we were the ones who delivered it to them?

Chris didn't need to hear the end of the question. "I'm not going to let anyone cut him up or anything, Brady."

"Yeah, I get that," I said. "*You* wouldn't. But remember the time the military put me and Cam in a glass cage underground? Because I do, and that sure as fuck wasn't fun."

Chris pressed his mouth into a thin line and then exhaled and dragged his fingers through his hair. "Yeah."

I didn't know if that was an acknowledgement or an apology. Neither did he probably.

He reached down for the tin cups beside the hybrid's cot. "Come on, you can help me with this."

THE NEAREST ALCOVE was back past our room. I looked in while we passed and everyone was sleeping. Not that I needed to look to know with the connection we shared, but human habits were hard to break. I followed Chris through the curving passageway to the alcove. He stopped when he reached it and stared at the wall for a while.

"It's creepy now, right?" I asked. "Like creepier than before. And it was creepy as fuck before, but now it's like every eyelash, every flake of skin you leave in there, the ship could use that to make a living, breathing thing."

"Nature isn't creepy," Chris said. "And this is just nature."

But he still hesitated.

"What nature have you been watching?" I asked him. "Back home, in Kopa, I once watched a gecko cannibalize another gecko right on my bedroom ceiling. Nature is fucked up. They get you in with those pictures of sunsets and golden leaves and shit, but it's all a lie. Nature is brutal and ugly and gross."

Chris's mouth twitched in the gloom. "Aren't you going to be a paramedic?"

That threw me. Because he wasn't mocking me for it. He wasn't saying I couldn't do it, that I was too dumb, or too old to start, or too poor. There was a joke in his words, but it wasn't on me.

"Maybe," I said. "In which case it's my professional opinion that nature is disgusting, and the human body is pretty fucking disgusting too."

"Well, I won't disagree with you there." Chris pressed his hand against the alcove, and the wall closed around him.

I waited, and wondered how long this would take. Would he wait for the entire alcove to fill up, or would he—

The walls opened again. Chris was crouching on the floor, his bare feet shining with goo, and the bottom of his trousers stuck to his calves like he'd been paddling through sludge. That answered that, I guessed.

He passed the two tin cups up to me, and rose to his feet.

We walked back toward the medbay.

"You really think this is what it needs?" I asked, eyeing the goo in the cups.

"I have no clue." Chris pulled up short suddenly, his expression tightening.

There was a Faceless standing in the door of the medbay. It turned its head when it saw us, and I felt a frisson of unease along the connection. It wasn't Kai-Ren—it wasn't *immediate* enough to be him, somehow; it didn't feel right—but it was one of the hive.

Chris moved forward. "What do you want?" he asked the Faceless.

The Faceless didn't move.

As chatty as fucking ever.

Chris squared his shoulders. "What are you doing here? Did you touch it? Kai-Ren said I could have it. He gave me his word."

I could see Chris's face reflected ghostly-pale in the mask of the Faceless.

"Did you touch it?" Chris asked again, lifting his chin like he was really going to fucking square up to a Faceless if he got an answer he didn't like. His anger thrummed through him, through all of us, and the Faceless tilted its head as it regarded him.

And then it moved out of the doorway.

Chris hurried inside.

I followed him, more slowly, and watched as the Faceless turned and walked away. A moment before it was swallowed by the gloom, I thought I saw another one standing there.

Saw it, but I couldn't feel it.

The Stranger?

The last time I'd seen him, he'd been standing over Harry, ready to hurt him. But now, when I blinked into the darkness that was barely softened by the weird gelatinous lights that bobbed in the walls, the Stranger was swallowed up by the black and I wasn't sure if he'd been there at all, or if he was just the manifestation of my fears.

I stepped inside the medbay and passed Chris the tin cups.

"There was another one out there, I think. I saw it, but I couldn't feel it."

Chris's focus was on the hybrid. "I don't think they touched him."

The hybrid's chest was still rising and falling shallowly. Its eyes were still dark slits. It was still creepy as fuck, so situation normal there, right? I grabbed Doc's stethoscope so I could do the obs while Chris rubbed the fluid into its skin and dribbled some down its throat.

Its obs were unchanged from the last hour.

"You really think they were going to hurt it?" I ventured at last.

"That Faceless didn't exactly read warm and fuzzy to me," Chris muttered, massaging fluid into the webbing between the hybrid's fingers. The skin looked dry and cracked there. Maybe the fluid would help. "You?"

"They're Faceless," I said. "I never get anything off them except the urge to run and scream."

Chris snorted, but it sounded a bit like agreement.

I drew a deep breath and tried to force myself to relax a little. It hadn't worked for the past three months, and it wasn't likely to start working now, but when had I ever learned a lesson quickly?

"Do you really think that one day you'll be able to talk—"

Except I never got the question out, because at that moment the Faceless ship made an echoing sound like the song of a distressed whale, and then a sudden shudder ran through her, and through me, and through all of us. And the hybrid, who hadn't moved since Kai-Ren had torn it from its sac, sat bolt upright on the cot, it's dark eyes shining in the gloom, and then opened its mouth to suck in a wet, rasping breath that felt as loud as a scream.

CHAPTER 10

"Brady, go!" Chris told me.

The corridor between the medbay and our room had never felt as long before. It was dark, still dark, but the weird low lights floating between the walls were purple and red, in tones I'd never seen before, and the ship shuddered around me. She was hurt. I knew it without seeing it, because I could feel it. She was hurt.

She made that sound again—whale song—and it reverberated through her, through me. I felt it bone deep.

The reappearance of the Stranger? The other ship that had drawn up alongside ours? An attack. Somewhere, our ship had been breached, and she was bleeding into the black. She had been breached and boarded.

I felt them, or rather I felt *our* Faceless pushing back against them. Our human brains weren't built for this. We were so incompatible and so out of sync with the Faceless. We couldn't process the signals we received—we could barely even describe them—but we could feel the echoes of them. We were the insects who skated in the water tension on the surface of the pond. We didn't know what was happening above us or below. We existed in a narrow place. We never saw the rock get thrown, who threw it or where it landed, but we felt the ripples in the surface of the pond.

We could feel them now.

Other consciousnesses, other entities, prickled at the edges of my awareness like static. They weren't part of our network, our connection, but the Faceless that now moved onto our ship used the same method to communicate as Kai-Ren and his hive did, but on a slightly different frequency. They were interference, or feedback, or a radio squelch, or something. They were there, and I could feel them.

My consciousness washed up against the wall of their cold hostility even as I struggled to breathe. I could feel my fear, and Chris's, and Cam's and Lucy's and everyone's, and behind all of that I could also feel something new: Kai-Ren's uncertainty. It wasn't sharp enough to call it fear, or maybe he wasn't smart enough to process it that way. Whatever this was, it was unprecedented.

Cam had called him the Faceless battle regent once because he was their leader, not just of his own hive, but because he directed other hives as well, or held some authority over them that he'd won in previous battles with whatever the hell else lived out here in the black. And now, for the first time, another hive—the Stranger's—had pushed back. Had refused to accept his authority. Had attacked him. It had seen the hybrid—that sign of Kai-Ren's weakness—and attacked.

And Kai-Ren hadn't been expecting that.

Kai-Ren had promised to take us home, but how much was his word worth in the face of a mutiny?

I turned into our room. Lucy tore herself from Cam's grasp and flung herself toward me. I caught her and held her tight. Her fear thrummed like a high musical note played on frayed strings. It reverberated, and wavered, and hung in the air between us. So did mine, probably.

"What's going on out there?" Andre asked.

I shook my head. "I know as much as you do. I haven't seen anything. But I think we're under attack."

Our ship was hurting, and there were Faceless here who weren't a part of this hive. What else was there to understand?

"Okay," Cam said. "We need to get to one of the alcoves. We need armor, in case of actual fighting, or decompression."

"And then what?" Harry asked.

"Then we hole up somewhere," Cam said, "and stay the hell out of the way." He looked at me. "Where's Chris?"

"With the hybrid."

Cam nodded. "Okay. Let's go. Andre, you and me will take point. Brady and Doc, stick with Lucy. Harry, you're watching our backs."

Watching for what, though? If the Faceless found us and wanted us dead, then we were dead. But I kept my mouth shut, because Cam knew this stuff better than me. The military taught their officers how to lead, how to take the initiative. They never taught that shit to the rest of us. They only taught their enlisted men how to die. We picked up the cynicism for free along the way. And some of us had a head start in that way before we were even conscripted. Some of us were born fucking cynical.

The nearest alcove from our room was the one Chris and I had visited earlier with our tin cups. We started toward it, moving slowly and quietly in the darkness.

The Faceless ship had been built—or born, or hatched, or whatever—on a spiral. The curve of the corridors meant that it wasn't just the darkness that obscured our vision. It also meant there were no cross-passages to use as cover if we needed it. We were exposed.

My fear sharpened as we followed the corridor up. I heard a sudden screech of something in my head, a soundless scream as though the creature who had been making it had been pulled underwater in front of me and my mind had filled in the sound from just the shape of its mouth, in the absence of any actual sound. Then a rush of dizziness washed over me, there and gone in the blink of an eye, and everything felt off kilter somehow when it was done.

There was...

There was an empty space somewhere.

Somehow.

And then it wasn't empty anymore.

I didn't understand what it was I was feeling.

"Did..." Harry whispered from behind us. "Did anyone else feel that?"

"Someone's missing," Lucy whispered back. "One of the Faceless is gone."

God. That was it. One of the Faceless from our hive had been killed. Snuffed out and gone, and our connection had readjusted.

When I was a kid, my dad used to take me hunting for eels in the mangroves. Dad knew the trick of how to spot them from the tiny bubbles that appeared in the brackish water, and then suddenly he'd thrust his gnarled hands down into that stinking, sticky mud and pull a wriggling eel free, and I'd watch as the water rushed back in to fill the hole he'd made. It only took a minute or two before the bubbles died away and the sediment settled again and it was as though nothing had ever happened.

"Keep moving," Cam said, his voice low. "Come on."

I held Lucy's hand tightly in mine as we continued up the sloping corridor.

The alcove was maybe fifteen or twenty meters away from us when we felt it: from somewhere in the heart of the ship, fighting. Everything we knew was because we felt it. There wasn't any sound.

Back on Defender Three, when they'd made us watch the footage of Cam getting taken by Kai-Ren, there hadn't been any sound then either. They'd cut the audio so we couldn't hear Cam screaming. But the Faceless, when they fought, were silent. And we knew why now. What use was sound when they could communicate via their connection?

But if there was no sound, there was still a cacophony of fear, of surprise, of the rush of adrenaline, of sudden sharp pain, of rage. And the connection spiked higher and higher with every emotion the Faceless experienced as they fought the intruders. Through it all, Kai-Ren's mind was a solid presence. In that twisting chaotic tangle of threads, he was the anchor line.

I couldn't tell which hive was winning.

"Okay," Cam said as we reached the alcove. "Let's go. Lucy, Brady."

I took a breath and stepped into the alcove with Lucy, and the opening oozed shut behind us.

It had been a long time since I'd used one of these for anything but food and sleep. I looked up, waiting for the weird slimy tubes to drop down and cover us in fluid that would harden into Faceless armor, but nothing happened.

"Come on," I told the ship. "Come on."

And still nothing happened.

Jesus fuck.

The sudden realization was as cold as ice.

In all our time here, we'd had no control over the alcoves at all, had we? It had been Kai-Ren and the other Faceless who'd somehow got the alcoves to do what we needed, through whatever interface they used. The ship wasn't connected to us in the same way it was connected to them. We needed an intermediary, and all our intermediaries were currently fighting for control of the ship.

"Why isn't it working?" Lucy asked me, her eyes large in the gloom. "Brady? Why isn't anything happening?"

"I don't know." Her hand shook in mine. "I don't know."

I pushed on the door to the alcove and it peeled open.

"Nothing's happening," I told the others. "We can't get it to start."

"Shit," Andre said. "What now?"

Cam dragged a hand through his hair. "Okay, then we'll hole up somewhere and hide, and hope Kai-Ren wins."

It wasn't much of a plan, but it was all we had.

WE MET Chris and the hybrid coming up the corridor as we were heading back down. Chris was half-leading, half-carrying the hybrid. Its eyes were open, and its mouth was, but it still looked as weak as hell and half dead.

"What's going on?" he asked us. "Where's your armor?"

So he'd had the same thought to get to an alcove.

"They don't work without the Faceless," Cam said.

Chris raised his eyebrows.

Another hurried trip to the alcove and we learned that they didn't work with the hybrid either. So much for that.

We headed back up, away from the fighting and, we hoped, away from the attention of the hostile Faceless who had boarded the ship.

IT WAS a tight squeeze in the recess Cam and I frequented, with all of us and the hybrid, but it was about the farthest we could be from the core of the ship, and as far as Cam and I had figured in the past there was no real reason for any of the Faceless to come up here. Kai-Ren did sometimes, but that was to find us. To talk to us sometimes, and sometimes just to watch us. He was interested in the things we did when we were together. Or, more precisely, he was interested in the things we felt when we were together. He drank in our emotions like they were an intoxicant. Humanity fascinated Kai-Ren, and look where it had led him.

Did the Faceless feel regret?

I sat on the floor, my back against the wall, with Lucy wedged between me and Cam, and wondered how long the battle would last. I also wondered if there would be a time, looking back, when I'd regret my impatience. Because right now I didn't know if Kai-Ren was winning or not. An hour in the future, or two, or three, and maybe I'd know for sure and wish I was still in a place in time when I didn't. Sometimes it felt like I'd spent my whole life just waiting for things to be over, only to find out that shit was a hell of a lot worse on this side of them.

Lucy curled up against me, and I put an arm around her skinny shoulders. I thought of that song she liked when she was a baby. The one my dad sang to her as a lullaby. Lucy called it the sasi sasi song. It was in a language we didn't know. I don't know where Dad had learned it.

I hummed a bar of it and Lucy hugged me tighter.

Across from us, the hybrid tilted its head and looked at me.

I looked away. I looked at Cam instead.

The first time I saw Cam I thought he was a corpse. Crazy, how much he'd given me. How well he knew me, how much he saw when he looked at me, and yet he'd never taken a step away from me, not even when I'd pushed. Not even when everyone who even cared for him a bit must have told him he was fucking insane for staying with someone like me. Cam was a rock, and I was the ocean that broke over him again and again.

Chris had said that Cam had found the thing he was looking for.

Crazy that it was me.

I love you, Cam, I told him silently, and didn't give a fuck if the rest of them heard it too. Wasn't like it was a secret anyhow. *You're my heartbeat.*

It washed back to me like an echo: *Love you too, Brady.*

There were worst things than facing the end with the people you loved, right? And here I was with Cam and Lucy and Doc. That was more than a lot of people got. I hoped it wouldn't hurt, and I hoped that Lucy wouldn't be afraid, but there were worse things. I'd already got a story much bigger than I'd had any right to. Kids from Kopa weren't supposed to end up floating in nebulas. Kids from Kopa weren't supposed to lift their gazes from the red dirt to begin with, but here I was.

"We're going to make it," Cam said. "We are."

And he sounded so certain.

I would never understand where Cam found his faith, not if we were together for an eternity.

When I was a kid, the school in Kopa was run by some religious group, because the government was done throwing money at the reffos. Every morning we had to press our hands together and pray. Mostly I prayed that someone would share their lunch with me. Anyhow, I learned to shut my mouth and bow my head, and listen to the words the teachers said that promised that somewhere out in the universe, someone was watching us, making sure things turned out the way he wanted, making rules for us to follow. Rules and order, so that everything made sense.

Which was the gap between religion and philosophy.

Which was the gap between hope and experience.

Which was the gap between Cam and me.

Then again, I'm pretty sure Cam's introduction to faith hadn't been the same as mine.

"Usually I'd tell you that was bullshit," I whispered to him over the top of Lucy's head.

He raised his eyebrows. "Usually?"

"Yeah. But it turns out you're a lot smarter than me, LT, so maybe this time I'll believe you."

His mouth quirked. "Good."

"Good," I echoed, and if there was some higher power up there who was really directing all the bullshit in the universe, I hoped it was watching out not just for those of us jammed into the dark little recess at the top of the Faceless ship—I hoped it was watching out for Kai-Ren too, because Kai-Ren was our only way home.

"WE NEED A PLAN," Chris said after a while. Always the officer, always the leader. Always thinking three steps ahead. "If Kai-Ren loses this, then they'll come for the hybrid, and then they'll come for us."

Contaminants and abominations.

"We can't use the alcoves," Andre said. "And we don't have any weapons. If the Faceless have sidearms, we don't know where they are, and we don't know if we could even use them."

"I'm not taking about weapons," Chris said. He nodded toward Lucy. "I'm talking about armor."

"We already tried that," Harry said, his forehead furrowed.

"No, I'm talking about the best armor on this ship," Chris said.

"Something that can withstand the vacuum of space for extended periods of time. I'm talking about the pods."

The pods. Cam had been sealed in one once, and it had carried him through the black all the way safely back to Defender Three. And I'd been in one once, and it had healed my broken, shattered body.

"We can't get the alcoves to work," Cam said. "What makes you think we could get the pods to work?"

"Because the pods are different," Chris said. "Nothing else here has *writing*. Look, nothing else here looks manufactured, right? Nothing looks like tech. It all looks like, well, evolution. But the pods are tech, aren't they? Writing doesn't just spontaneously occur in nature."

I thought of the first time I'd seen Cam. Or rather, the first time I'd heard about Cam from Branski, that fucking asshole. How his eyes had lit up like he was sharing a horror story that he knew would give us all nightmares for years. *"He's in water or something... And, Jesus, his skin! They wrote all over it. Like tattoos or something. And it fucking glows."*

And later in Doc's medbay on Defender Three I'd seen it for myself. How the letters shone against his skin. How—the most terrifying thing of all—when I'd touched the opaque surface of the pod Cam, pale as a corpse, had mirrored my movement and pressed his hand against mine. The slimy skin of the sac had slid between our palms. And the writing on his skin, we learned much later, hadn't been tattoos at all. It had been projected there by something inside the pod.

I gazed across the recess at Chris.

"He's right," I said. "The pods are different. But that still doesn't mean we could use them. They might be locked to us."

"But they aren't," Doc said slowly. "Not necessarily, anyway. We fucked the pod up back with Cam because we didn't know what we were doing. But it had been designed that we could operate it."

"Yeah, but we still don't know what we're doing," I pointed out. "We don't know how to work them at all."

"It's better than waiting here to get killed," Chris said.

"Is it?" I asked. "Because what if we manage to open then, and use them, and somehow not drown ourselves? What if we even managed to use them to get off this ship? Do you know the way home, Chris? Because I sure as shit don't."

We'd be adrift.

How long would it take until the pods couldn't sustain us anymore?

How long would it take to die out there?

Which was stupid. It'd be like me climbing into the cockpit of a Hawk and worrying about crashing it, when I didn't even know how to start the fucking engine.

Cam shifted beside me. "Maybe," he said, holding Chris's gaze. "If things go bad, we might as well try. But only as a last resort, because Brady's right. The chances it would work would are so small it wouldn't even be worth it unless we were sure our only other option was dying."

Chris was silent for a moment, and then he nodded. "Yeah. Worst case scenario. But it won't do us any good to debate it from here if things go badly. We need to be with the pods, to at least see if we can ever power them up."

"How many Faceless between us and the pods?" Harry asked, his voice rasping.

Chris shook his head and shrugged. "Only one way to find out."

THE FACELESS SHIP WAS SILENT, but the anger and the adrenaline rush of the battle ran on a constant feedback loop in our skulls. Spikes of pain, of fear, were like blasts of static in our heads. And sometimes, more than once, we felt that same dizzying sensation of sudden loss—and of that hole immediately being filled in again. The Faceless felt no grief for the fallen. The hive barely even noticed the loss of one drone.

I thought of my dad and how acutely I still missed him and

how his loss was written in my bones, and in everything I did. A day didn't go by when I didn't think of him. And I thought of how my grief and my fear for Lucy had captured Kai-Ren's attention in the first place.

I wondered which one of us was the most incomprehensible to the other. The most alien.

We made our way carefully down toward the core of the ship. Everything seemed dimmer. There were fewer lights drifting in the walls, and the fluid itself seemed darker than usual. The ship was hurt. Was she dying too?

Chris and Doc carried the hybrid between them, his thin arms held across their shoulders. His pale feet dragged more than stepped, but his eyes were open now. They were dark and wide and fearful, just like mine.

Cam and Harry led the way, and Andre and I brought up the rear. I held Lucy's hand tightly. It was warm and damp with sweat. She was quiet. Her face was pinched. But she didn't even stumble as we moved forward through the dimly-lit curving passageway of the ship.

As we moved toward the fighting.

"If anything happens," I whispered to her, "run back to where we just were, okay?"

She nodded, and squeezed my hand more tightly.

We kept moving, right up until we didn't. Cam and Harry had stopped, and I craned my head to see.

"It's okay," Cam said. "Keep moving."

There was a dead Faceless lying in the corridor. His mask had been removed. His eyes were covered in a white film. His yellowish skin was stained black around his throat, and over one cheek, like someone had spat ink over him. And then I realized that no, it wasn't a stain. It was necrosis, or something like it. His skin had been ruptured in several places, punctured, and the flesh around it had turned black.

Venom. It had to be venom.

I looked at Doc and Chris, and at the way the hybrid was slung between them. The hybrid's fingers curled around their shoulders, and I thought of claws digging into their flesh and wondered how long it would take Faceless venom to kill a human. And then I thought of every time that Kai-Ren had run his hands over my skin, and of how the Stranger had prodded my stomach, and how each time I'd been staring death in the face. I'd thought of Kai-Ren as a god once, hadn't I? A god who could strike any one of us down on a whim.

I held Lucy's hand tightly as we passed the dead Faceless.

There was a voice in the back of my head—mine, for once—that told me we weren't going to make it to the pods. That told me we'd be caught here, in a curving corridor with nowhere to take cover and that the Stranger's Faceless would kill us, but whatever was happening in the rest of the ship was keeping all the Faceless busy.

My heart was beating out of my chest by the time we descended to the bay where the pods were kept, and the doors shut behind us, the sticky seams sealing closed.

There were six pods here, and seven of us plus the hybrid. It didn't matter, because Cam and I had shared a pod before anyway. There was plenty of room. But mostly it didn't matter because we had no way of getting the pods to work, let alone launching them.

And then it *really* didn't matter, because we wouldn't be launching them into some tranquil sea anyway.

"Holy *fuck!*" Harry exclaimed from the one of the windows that looked out into the nebula.

I look past him just in time to see a Faceless ship being torn apart by a massive explosion. It was colossal. It was blinding.

And it was close enough that the shockwave hit us like a tsunami.

CHAPTER 11

"Brady? Brady!"

The blood roared in my skull as I forced my eyes open to find Cam on his knees beside me, his hands hovering like he was afraid to touch.

"Are you hurt?"

"Gimme...gimme a second." I blinked, and the bay slowly came back into focus. It didn't look like anything had changed, except I was lying on the floor. I took a slow breath, testing for pain, but there was nothing sharp. Just a dull ache. I was winded, that was all.

I turned my head to look for everyone else. Harry had a bright ribbon of blood sliding down his temple, and was wincing as Doc prodded at him, but everyone else seemed okay. The hybrid was on the floor as well, skinny limbs twitching like spider's legs as he drew them back toward himself and huddled over.

"Lucy?" I asked.

She appeared over Cam's shoulder. "I'm okay."

"Okay." I gave Cam my hand, and let him pull me up. I fought against a wave of dizziness, and held on to Cam until it faded. "What the fuck just happened?"

"There was another ship coming," Lucy said, e
"Then it *exploded*!"

I held Cam's gaze.

We were in serious trouble here. If the rest of the Faceless were turning against Kai-Ren, how long could he hold them off? How long would we survive this?

"Did we do that?" Chris asked, his gaze fixed on the window of the bay where, outside, the Faceless ship drifted like an asteroid field, broken apart into dark jagged pieces against the soft cloud of the nebula. "Did our ship do that?"

He turned back to face us, a crazy half-smile on his face like he'd just seen something wonderful. Faceless weaponry. He'd wanted to know about it from the start, and he'd just been given a front row seat to the light show. The same light show that had destroyed most of the major cities on Earth, but Chris wasn't seeing anything except fireworks, was he?

"We've got more incoming," he said. "I hope our ship's got more where that came from."

Here we were in the target zone for every other Faceless ship in the fucking nebula, and he was talking like he was a *spectator*. How did he do that? How did he put enough distance between himself and what was happening? I envied him that, and it was a sudden, sharp emotion that I didn't like. Because I froze when the universe was exploding around me, but somehow Chris Varro stepped forward to watch in wonder.

"A plan would be good, Chris," Cam said, reaching out to squeeze my hand for a moment.

"Right," Chris said, moving away from the window at last. "The pods. The pods are the back-up plan, right?" He touched one, running his fingers down the shiny black carapace. "If we can get them to work. Otherwise, they're useless to us. Harry?" He nodded at the pod.

Harry clambered up into one, lying back so that he was lower than the carapace.

Nothing happened.

No skin grew over the pod. No fluid filled it. No lights shone.

"There's no buttons or anything in here," Harry said, his voice echoing from the confines of the carapace.

Great. We couldn't get armor, and we couldn't get the pods to activate.

Andre began to feel around the seams on the exterior of the pod.

"So much for the back-up plan," Chris said. "We need Kai-Ren."

Andre helped haul Harry out of the pod. "I think Kai-Ren's a little busy right now."

"Yeah," Chris said. "Well, we're locked out of everything on this ship, and we need armor, and we need those pods operational, so we need Kai-Ren."

Always so fucking focused, Chris Varro. Always the guy who knew what the goal was, what the objective was. Didn't matter how many obstacles were in the way—Chris would just push right through them, wouldn't he, with a dash of that arrogance they handed out in spades in officer training and a hell of a lot of cocky self-confidence that was his and his alone. And he'd do it with a smile, even if he got everyone else killed on the way.

Except as much as I hated to admit it, he also had a point. We needed Kai-Ren. Our chances of surviving this without him, and without Faceless technology, weren't exactly stellar.

"So what's the plan?" Cam asked, his gaze steady.

Chris exhaled slowly. "We split up. Andre and Harry, you guys stay here in the bay with Doc and Lucy and the hybrid. Keep the doors shut, if you can."

"And if we can't?" Harry asked.

Chris just shook his head slightly and didn't answer that. He didn't have to. He looked over to Cam and me. "Cam and Brady, we'll go and find Kai-Ren. Your connection with him is stronger than mine. And he listens to both of you. We might need that."

"You think?" I asked. "Middle of his ship exploding and we're going to ask him to worry about his fucking house pets? Yeah, that'll go down well."

"With that attitude, sure," Chris said. He'd learned Cam's

trick of not rising to my bait. "We need to find Kai-Ren and help him win this."

"We?" Cam asked. There was a tone in the word that was almost a laugh, that's how ludicrous this all was. "Chris, there's no 'we' in this fight. It's Faceless against Faceless. We *can't* be in it. We literally have no way of engaging. We have no armor and no weapons. We can't operate their technology. What are we going to do? Slap them around a bit?"

Except *can't* wasn't a word that Chris Varro had ever listened to in his life. He wouldn't have been here otherwise.

"Listen, Cam," Chris said.

Cam's brows tugged together. "What?"

"No, *listen*," Chris said. "Listen to the bond. It's... the network is getting smaller. Kai-Ren's Faceless are *losing*."

Fear settled deep in my gut, and a shiver ran through me. Chris was right. I knew it instinctively. I *felt* it. There were fewer Faceless in our connection than before. The gaps had been filled in, but it was like painting over the cracks in a wall. The paint was too thin, and behind it the wall was starting to crumble. Soon the whole thing would collapse.

"And if Kai-Ren loses," Chris said, "then we're all dead as well. So we either wait for that to happen, or we help him. We need weapons and armor, and if those won't save us we need the pods. Otherwise we're sitting ducks. But if he gives us access to their tech—*all* their tech—then we're *reinforcements*."

So he had a point. Whole fucking universe was on fire outside. Maybe Kai-Ren would actually appreciate the backup.

Chris took our collective stunned silence as agreement. Or maybe he didn't, but he pressed on anyway because he knew it was the best he was going to get.

"We've got incoming still," he said. "And we've got at least one other Faceless ship docked with us. Until that ship undocks, then I'd guess we're safe from being targeted by missiles, or whatever the fuck it was our ship used to take that other one out."

"You'd *guess*?" Harry asked, arching his brows. My attitude was catching.

"This whole fucking thing is nothing but guesswork, Harry," Chris said. "It has been since Earth."

Guesswork, dumb luck and recklessness. Jesus. We were humanity's finest, weren't we? I probably could have laughed at that if we weren't so close to getting killed. Chris would probably laugh at it anyway, because what else was there to do?

You pushed that same rock up that same hill every fucking day, and one day it was bound to roll back and crush you. And at least your painful death would be a break in your usual routine, right? That thought was more bluster and bullshit than actual bravery, but it was enough. Bluster and bullshit had always carried me through before.

Cam looked to me.

I looked to Lucy, a thousand different thoughts swirling through my head and none of them good. But Chris was right. He was right.

"I'll be back soon, Lucy," I told her.

She nodded, her eyes wide, and I didn't need the Faceless connection between us to know that she didn't really believe me. Lucy was Kopa born and bred. She knew bullshit when she heard it. She also knew when the odds were stacked against us.

I looked to Cam and Chris. They were expecting me to be the one to dissent, the one to refuse, the one to break. Fuck that though. If I was going to die, then I'd die fighting. I'd die angry, same way as I'd been born. I squared my shoulders. "Let's go find Kai-Ren."

KAI-REN WAS our savior-god and he was our destroyer-god. He could shield us or he could smite us, and there was no in-between. And the trick was, the trick had always been that we would never be able to tell the difference.

And maybe neither could he.

We'd come out here into the black to learn about the Faceless, to learn about the universe and our place in it. Shit, there was probably a part of Chris Varro who saw this whole thing as an exercise in philosophy as much as anything else—*"But what does it mean to be human?"*—except all we'd ever see, all we'd ever be, would be the shadows on the walls of the cave.

And now the shadows on the walls had become shapes inside them, moving, twisting, shifting in the walls like little bits of seaweed caught in the back-and-forth churn of the tide, and as I followed Cam and Chris down into the heart of the Faceless ship, I wondered what would happen if I broke my chains and turned around.

I wondered what I'd see.

And I wondered, with a sick, dizzy feeling, if I'd ever really left the pod that Kai-Ren had put me into that time when my body was broken. If maybe I was still there now, still drowning slowly, and everything that had happened since was nothing more than a simulation.

How was I supposed to know?

How was anyone?

"Brady," Cam said softly, holding his hand back for me.

I took it and squeezed it, and we continued down the corridor with the shifting shapes in the walls, glowing and pulsing, lighting our path.

I'd follow Cam into hell, probably.

And Cam, it turned out, would follow Chris.

There was no room here now for my petty jealousy. Maybe one day, if we survived this, I'd let it flare. Coax the embers of it into a flame. Wouldn't that be just like me? Cam and me and Lucy, safe back on Earth in our sunlit apartment, and I'd sabotage it all by accusing Cam of wanting to fuck Chris. And I knew he didn't. I'd been in his head. I *knew* it, but when the hell had I ever let the truth get in the way of my smart mouth? If Cam was following Chris into hell now, it was because it was our only option. It was because Chris was the officer in charge of this goat-fuck of a mission. It was because Cam trusted him. It had nothing to do with their past.

We followed the twisting thread of the corridor deeper into the heart of the Faceless ship.

The connection in my head buzzed with static, with sharp bursts of white noise, with things I couldn't untangle, but none of them were good. The connection hummed like a swarm of angry wasps in my skull, scrambling to defend their nest.

And then we saw it: the tall black figure of a Faceless at the curve of the corridor. The glowing lights in the walls made shifting patterns across his inky, featureless mask, like sunlight on water.

"Is he one of ours?" Chris asked in an undertone.

He couldn't tell. Neither could I. If the connection was like a radio signal, then there was too much interference right now.

Chris moved forward.

The Faceless turned its mask toward us.

"Where is Kai-Ren?" Chris asked it.

The Faceless tilted its head, like a dog asking a question.

"Not one of ours," Chris said, a thrill of fear running through him and washing back between Cam and me.

The Faceless stared at him.

Insects, I remembered. We were insects, or house pets. We were *nothing* to the Faceless. This Faceless wasn't hunting us. We were beneath its consideration while Kai-Ren's Faceless were still alive.

In *theory*.

Chris had obviously reached the same conclusion.

"Keep moving," he said. I felt his fear, felt him steel himself against it, and watched as he stepped past the Faceless.

The Faceless turned its head to watch him go.

In theory we were beneath the consideration of the Faceless. In practice I wanted to piss myself.

Cam held my hand tightly, keeping himself between me and the Faceless. He tugged us forward. I clamped my jaw to stop it from trembling as we moved past the silent Faceless. I glanced at its mask, at the reflected colors that swirled there like an oil slick, and sensed nothing behind it but a void.

It hissed lowly, but made no move toward us.

We rounded the curve, the corridor opening up ahead of us, and saw two more of them.

Two more of the Stranger's Faceless.

Chris moved toward them, intending to pass them like we had the other one. One of them shot a hand out, and made a curious sound, and Chris pulled up short.

No.

No, we were on their radar now. Not a threat, but no longer nothing either. We weren't invisible anymore, and we could taste the menace in the humid air.

"Okay," Chris said softly. "Let's back it up before they get angry."

Cam and I turned back and moved up the corridor. The first Faceless came into view again. His mask was still turned toward us, and as we reappeared in his field of vision he splayed his fingers. And maybe it was a meaningless gesture, but all I could do was think of claws.

Cam and I retreated again, bumping back into Chris.

We were caught between the Faceless now, in the narrowest of spaces where we were still out of sight. A step or two in either direction would take us back into their field of vision.

I looked hopelessly for a door.

"This is bullshit," I whispered, my voice shaking. "There's got to be a better way to—"

Fuck, we were dumb shits.

What had I been thinking since the moment we came aboard? How paltry words like *doors* and *windows* and *walls* were for what we'd encountered here on the Faceless ship. The usual definitions didn't apply.

The walls.

Did the walls count as tech? Had we been locked out of those?

I pulled my hand free from Cam's, and pressed it against the wall. It bowed, just like the one around the hatchery had, and then it gave, and my hand was inside it.

"I think I found a shortcut," I said, my heart thumping.

I leaned slowly into the wall, and it opened up to accept me. A warm, sticky sensation crept over my skin as the wall oozed closed around me.

If the wall around the hatchery was a thin membrane between chambers, then this wall was an artery. I kept my eyes shut, and fought against the panic of my near-drowning while the fluid burned my lungs. And then I was breathing again, for certain values of breathing at least, and I opened my eyes again. The fluid stung for a moment and then I could see again.

Everything was weird and murky, like a sand-churned ocean.

A glowing orange something bobbed in front of my blurry vision for a moment before it was carried away on the tide that tugged me forward too. I was strong enough to prevent getting swept away, but I was glad that the current—the *bloodstream?*—was heading in the direction we needed. It'd be hard work to fight against it.

Coming back again was a problem for future Brady, right? If that guy was still alive in an hour or so.

I turned my head and saw Cam and Chris were already inside with me. As I watched, Cam raised his hand slowly and something shaped like a stringy jellyfish, or a clump of seaweed—or maybe some kind of filamentous bacteria magnified by about a million degrees—brushed against his fingers before bumping into me and then flowing past me.

I turned my head to look back out into the corridor. I watched the two Faceless round the corner through the opaque lens of the wall. What was that saying? Through a glass darkly. That was from the Bible, I think, and I guessed it meant the same as watching the shadows on a cave wall.

Except we were those shadows now, weren't we? Me and Cam and Chris, and the Faceless didn't even glance at us as we slipped past them, letting the tide pull us deeper and deeper into the heart of the ship.

WE FOUND Kai-Ren in the center of the ship, in the core, or the heart, or whatever that strange place was where the lights gathered in the walls like Christmas, like fireflies, and the twisting banyan roots of the ship's veins and arteries were twined as close together as brambles. Kai-Ren lay where he had fallen, sprawled backwards across the corpse of another Faceless. His mask was split, and his death-white face stared up at us. There was a cut on his face, bisecting his hollow cheek. It was leaking pale fluid, as thick as pus.

I thought he was dead, and in that moment my heart stopped, and I *hated* him. I hated him for bringing us out here, further into the black than we ever should have gone, and I hated him for promising to take us home again. And I hated him most of all for all the times I'd thought he was a god, or at least some invincible nightmare, when he was as fucking mortal as any other weak creature who ever crawled in the dirt.

I hated him for failing us.

And slowly, Kai-Ren's yellow eyes blinked.

"Kai-Ren?" Cam asked, dropping to his knees beside him. He reached out and put a hand on his chest.

Kai-Ren's response whispered down our connection, faint and broken: "Cam-Ren."

My stomach twisted, and a fear deeper than any I'd ever known caught me. Was he dying? I was no Zarathustra and this was not a Nietzschean moment. If God was dead I only cared because it meant that I was dead too, and so was Lucy and Cam and every other human being on this ship.

Kai-Ren's chest rose as he sucked in a wet-sounding breath, and it sounded laborious. It sounded almost final.

No.

Every cell in my body screamed the word even while I was frozen in shock.

No, Kai-Ren wasn't allowed to die, because he'd promised us he'd take us home. He *owed* us that.

"We need to get him to the pod bay," I said, my voice rasping. "We need to get him *healed*."

Cam and Chris exchanged a look. It was a look that said they'd made the same calculations I had and they didn't like the result. But what choice did we have? Backs against the wall, what choice did we have?

This was a battle we were too small to fight, and it was a battle that the Stranger was winning. We needed to retreat. We needed to run, but we could only do that with Kai-Ren alive.

"Fuck this," I said. "I'm not dying in the black."

I crouched down on Kai-Ren's other side, and gripped his arm.

Between the three of us we hauled him more or less upright. His suit was slimy with goo, but whether that was because he'd been lying on the floor or whether it was because he it was coming from some wound, I had no idea. It was way too fucking gloomy inside the heart of the ship to see anything against the inky black of Kai-Ren's battle armor.

We half-carried, half-dragged Kai-Ren toward the nearest porous wall.

"Do we even know where this will take us though?" Chris asked, his brow furrowed.

"It's a circulatory system," I said. "It brought us down here, it'll take us up again."

Unless there were valves and chambers we couldn't get through, but we'd cross that bridge, or not, when we came to it.

"Besides, he's dying," I said. "And maybe the stuff in the walls might not even be the same as the stuff that fills the alcoves or the pods, but maybe it is, and maybe it will help!"

And maybe it would kill him quicker too, but at this point we didn't have much to lose. We were dead if we did nothing. Hell, we were probably dead anyway, but that didn't mean we could stop fighting. I wasn't sure Cam and Chris knew how, not while we still had room to move, and I sure as shit didn't. Not that I was smart about it like they were. I was just a stubborn little prick. Ask anyone. The universe could lock me in a concrete box and I'd still be kicking the walls until I died. And maybe that was what I brought to the team—since it sure as hell wasn't knowledge, or experience, or even optimism. Maybe all I brought was all I'd been born with: the mongrel in me. And Cam brought the pragmatism, apparently.

"We're out of options here, Chris," he said.

Chris nodded, a short sharp jerk of his chin, of his tightly clenched jaw, and we dragged Kai-Ren into the wall.

We leaned into it, a knot of interlacing limbs, and the wall swallowed us whole. And then the current caught us and carried us, lungs burning as we breathed the fluid in, deeper into the heart of the Faceless ship.

And, if we were lucky, maybe it would take us back up towards the pod bay, to Lucy and Doc and the others, to where we needed to be.

CHAPTER 12

WE PUSHED our way out of the walls *somewhere* in the Faceless ship. The current had pulled us deeper into the ship for a while, buffeting us together while we all clung to Kai-Ren like a life raft and globs of shining bits of *stuff* swirled past us. And then, as suddenly as getting dumped by a wave, we'd been dragged upward again. We'd ridden the current until we'd felt it begin to turn again, and pushed our way out of the walls into an interconnected honeycomb of rooms that served no purpose that was immediately apparent. Story of our fucking lives. The artery we'd been traveling through cut through the honeycombed rooms, but the rooms themselves were divided by walls that didn't appear to be porous. They shifted and stretched like ligaments. Maybe they were.

I knelt with Kai-Ren on the floor while Cam and Chris went in different directions to find a way out of our unexpected labyrinth. Kai-Ren's eyes were closed now. I kept a hand on his chest, just to feel the shaky rise and fall of his breathing and wondering, if it stopped, if there was anything I could do. Was my medic-level training worth shit with the Faceless? I didn't even know if he had a heart, let alone if CPR would do a fucking thing.

I closed my eyes briefly, and thought of the last guy I'd

performed CPR on. Mike Marcello. Hadn't done him any fucking good, had it?

"This way!" Chris yelled moments later.

Cam backtracked to find me, and we dragged Kai-Ren toward the sound of Chris's voice. Soon enough we found ourselves in what might have been the main spiral of the corridor. The ship was a fucking maze, but of course Chris knew his way. He'd been poking around in corners since the day we came aboard.

"This way," he said. He and Cam each took an arm of Kai-Ren's, leaving his feet for me. It was like dragging a corpse.

If he died, would we feel it?

We slowly descended down the spiral, and I was gratified when we passed the place that Cam and I sometimes snuck away to, and where we'd all hidden earlier before making our way to the pod bay. I knew where we were at last, though it seemed like a hundred years ago that we'd hidden there. Seemed like even longer since Cam and I had been there on our own, chasing our pleasure in private away from the curious appraisal of Kai-Ren and the Faceless.

Our journey to the pod bay felt laborious. It was terrifying too. I was afraid that every step that revealed another curve of the corridor would also reveal a Faceless. I tried to clear my mind and discover if any of Kai-Ren's Faceless were even still alive, but either my fear was broadcasting a blast of fear that drowned out the Faceless, or they were all dead. Or maybe I just couldn't hear them because it was Kai-Ren who'd held the connection together this entire time, and now he was dying it was broken.

There was too much we didn't understand about how any of this worked. I'd always known we were totally out of our depth, but now I looked at Chris's drawn face and thought that he was truly feeling it for the first time.

We were on our own.

And then we reached the pod bay, and rounded the entrance, and my world shattered.

I saw Andre first. The bulky shape of him, on his knees, his entire body shifting each time he performed chest compressions on the man lying on the floor.

Doc.

I froze again, Kai-Ren's boots slipping from my grasp and hitting the floor.

"Doc!" The name rasped out of me, but I still couldn't move, because this was a nightmare. This was a nightmare, and Andre and Doc were the only ones I could see in the bay, and what I was seeing was bad, so bad, but it didn't even *matter* because *where was Lucy?*

The universe was unraveling so quickly that it made me dizzy.

"Shit!" Cam was the first one to reach Andre and Doc. He dropped to his knees, taking over from Andre, and Andre sagged back, his bloody hands going to his stomach and pressing it tightly. He was hurt too, his shirt soaked in blood.

Moving forward was like walking underwater. Like trying to push against the currents inside the walls of the ship. I was slow and dumb and the only thing I could hear was the roar of blood in my skull.

My medic's training took over while the rest of me couldn't, except every part of my medic's training came down to one thing: do what you can until there's a doctor on scene. But what about when the doctor was the one lying on the ground not breathing?

"Keep going," I told Cam, and forced myself to look at Andre instead. "Show me."

Andre winced, and peeled his shirt up. The laceration went right across his abdomen, and it was deep. Doing the chest compressions on Doc had pushed his guts out the wound.

"Keep pressure on it," I told him. I needed to get to the medbay, except...

Except it wouldn't make a fucking difference. I could stitch him up, but this was the sort of injury that needed internal surgery, not just patching up. This was the sort of injury that might take hours or days to kill him, but it would happen. Morphine though. Doc had morphine in his supplies, so at least it wouldn't have to hurt.

"Just keep pressure on it." My eyes strung, and I held my hands over his. His were trembling. "Where's Lucy?"

"She's okay," Andre said softly, and how was it that he was the one comforting me? How was it that he cared for Lucy more than himself? It couldn't have just been because we'd shared memories. Because he'd once known what it felt like to wear a baby in a sling across his skinny chest and feel her heartbeat. It was that, but it was also more than that. Andre was a decent guy. He wasn't selfish. He was better than me. "The Faceless came. Not ours. They took Harry. We tried –we tried to stop them. Lucy hid."

"Lucy?" I called. "Lucy!"

Beside me, Cam was still doing chest compressions on Doc, and I still couldn't look at the face of the man who'd been the closest thing to a father to me since I'd been conscripted.

I saw a flash of movement over Andre's shoulder, and a small pale face appeared from underneath one of the pods. Lucy. She crawled out and behind her, like a naked, spindly spider, came the hybrid.

I fixed my gaze on that face that was a grotesque parody of mine.

Nothing to lose, I'd thought back when we'd found Kai-Ren.

That was still true, wasn't it?

I twisted around to look at Chris. He was crouching down over Kai-Ren. Kai-Ren's eyes were still closed. He was useless to us. I looked at Cam, his brow furrowed in concentration as he worked on Doc. And I looked at Andre, at his ashen face, and then down at where my bloody hands covered his.

Nothing to lose.

"Keep the pressure on it," I told Andre, and peeled my hands away from his. I rose to my feet, the muscles in my thighs aching from being crouched so awkwardly. "We're losing this fight. We need to win it."

We're losing *them*.

"How?" Cam asked, voice strained as he worked. "We can't use their tech, and we don't have any weapons of our own. Even if we did, there's nothing we have that could make a dent in Faceless armor."

The ship shook and shuddered as though she heard us, and rolled slowly like whale diving in the deep. The clouds of the nebula swirled in dizzying colors outside the window.

"The bond is like a virus, right?" I asked. "That's how we became a part of this. Kai-Ren infected you, you infected me, we passed it on to Lucy just be being close to her, and the others injected themselves with our blood to link themselves to the network. But we're not Faceless. This whole time we've been using the alcoves we thought we were controlling them, but we weren't, were we? We're locked out by default, but every time we've needed something, one of the Faceless has authorized it without us realizing it. How's that for a working theory?"

"Yeah," Chris said grimly. "That fits."

"So what's the lockout override? What if it's DNA? What if in order to work the tech, you need to be part of the hive bond *and* be Faceless?" I nodded at the hybrid. "He doesn't have the bond, but he has Faceless DNA. What if he was in our network? What if we could get him to operate this stuff for us?"

"Kai-Ren doesn't want him to be part of the hive," Cam reminded us.

Chris raised his eyebrows. "Kai-Ren's about to be dead."

Which was fair.

"So what if we tried that?" I asked. "Our bond plus his DNA? What have we got to lose at this point?"

And none of us had an answer for that.

I looked over at the hybrid who wore a twisted approximation of my face, and found him starting back at me with dark unblinking eyes. He hunkered down, sitting with his arms crossed over his chest and his twitching fingers splayed over his shoulders. There was a flutter in a muscle in his cheek that pulsed as fast as a frantic heartbeat.

I wondered if that meant he was scared too.

"Chris," I said. "Give me your knife."

The hybrid's skin wasn't as unyielding as the skin of a Faceless. It bowed under the pressure of the blade of Chris's pocketknife, and then split, and the hybrid let out a high-pitched keening sound and thrashed and thrashed and thrashed as Chris and I held him still. His blood wasn't yellow, but it wasn't quite red either. It was thicker than mine, and it was brown like sludge.

I thought of the dog I saw one time when I was a kid. How it got caught in barbed wire and made a sound just like that. It dug into my skull then, and it dug into it now. I fought the urge to cover my ears.

I was hurting him. The least I could do was be a witness to that and not turn away like a coward.

I glanced at Lucy, and her face was pale and tears slid down her cheeks.

I flipped the knife around in my grasp, and sliced my arm. It was a short, sharp sting that I hardly felt. Then I pressed the bloody wound against the matching one in the hybrid's arm while the hybrid thrashed again and tried to squirm away.

"Brady!" Lucy whispered loudly, her voice raw. "He's just a *baby*!"

Not a Faceless. Not a human. A baby. Is that how she saw him? Is that what he was?

I shot a look at Chris, and he pressed his mouth into a tight line.

And then it hit.

"Oh..." I was still pressing my bleeding wound against the hybrid's. "Shit. Do you feel that?"

When I was a kid, there was another kid who was my friend for a while. Morgan. He was just another snot-nosed dusty-footed Kopa kid, but we were best friends for a while. We were *brothers*. And Morgan took his dad's old fishing knife and one day we sat out by the side of the road that ran past his place, bare feet paddling in the red dirt, and we decided to become blood brothers. Morgan cut the pad of the thumb with the knife, and I remember how *red* his blood seemed against his dark skin—I'd never seen blood so red—and then I cut mine, and then we pressed our thumbs together and swore we were blood brothers.

When I was eight, I thought it would be magical, but all I got out of it was an infected thumb from that dirty fishing knife and a flogging from my step-mother because she was pissed that dad had to spend his pay on a tetanus shot for me instead of booze for her. But I'd thought, when Morgan's blood mixed with mine, that I'd feel something.

I felt something now.

The hybrid keened and thrashed, and he was scared, and so... so *alone*. His consciousness wasn't like the Faceless's. It wasn't so removed, so alien. The hybrid was an individual, and his mind crashed up against ours, new and discordant and chaotic and afraid.

Alone.

He'd woken up alone with Kai-Ren's fingers around his throat, while on the floor of the hatchery his clutch-mates lay in twisted, broken ways.

Alone.

Hands were on him, touching him, strange creatures who peered down at him as he lay on his cot. Their voices like dull murmurs. He was a thing in a box, an animal in a cage, a specimen behind thick glass. He didn't know what we were, and he didn't know what he was. The only thing he knew was fear.

Alone, except now we were flooding his mind with images of strange places, of people, of thoughts and memories and emotions, pouring them into him until he was sinking under the weight of them, and he didn't understand us, and he didn't know what any of these things meant, and he was drowning, panicked and afraid.

"Do you feel that?" I asked again, and, overwhelmed by the his fear, by his loneliness, I then forward and placed my hands on either side of the hybrid's face. Blood slid down my forearm. I left a smeared thumbprint of it on the hybrid's cheek. "It's okay. It's okay. It's okay."

The same soothing nonsensical tone I'd once used to calm Lucy when she was small and afraid and crying.

"It's okay," I told the hybrid, holding his dark gaze. "You're okay. Do you understand me? You're okay."

Middle of a fucking Faceless space battle we were currently losing, but sure, he was okay.

Chris threw me a wry look as that thought passed through my mind.

"We're all fucked if this doesn't work," I said, sharp-toothed fear gnawing at my guts. "We're all totally fucked."

"Situation normal then," Chris said, raising his eyebrows like he was daring me to have a breakdown right here and now. Daring me to falter when I could chose to move forward instead. Daring me to forget I was a stubborn little asshole who never went down without a fight. I could feel his grudging respect, warm as an embrace, when I lifted my chin and glared back at him.

He flashed me a smile. "Come on, let's see if this will actually work."

We hauled the hybrid to his feet, and pulled him over to the nearest pod.

"Please," I said, not even knowing how much he understood. "Please make it work. Please."

For Doc, and for Andre, and even for Kai-Ren who might still be our only way home.

The hybrid stared blankly at the pod.

I lifted my bloody hands and ran them over the pod's strange carapace. "Make it work, please."

The hybrid stared, and then raised his hands and slid them over the path mine had followed. My breath caught, and then—

A small row of lights at the side of the pod blinked on, and the pod thrummed as power ran through it.

Relief almost overwhelmed me, but we weren't in the clear yet. "Cam!" I yelled. "Cam, get him over here!"

Chris ran back to help, and between the two of them they lifted Doc and carried him to the pod. It took the three of us to lift him high enough to topple him in, and I grimaced at the indignity of it. But also, fuck indignity. This could save him.

The muggy air over the pod seemed to shimmer for a moment, and then the skin began to grow outward from the upper edges of the gleaming carapace, forming the sac. I stood on my toes and watched as fluid began to fill the pod.

I was either watching Doc drown, or I was watching him heal.

I turned away, grabbing the hybrid by the hand and drawing him along to the next pod. We wrestled Kai-Ren into that one.

Then the third.

"This gonna work?" Andre asked, wincing as we helped him climb in.

"I don't know," I said. I clenched his hand tightly as he lay down. He spasmed in pain. "Hope so."

"Yeah," Andre said faintly. "Me too."

"Good luck," Cam said, squeezing his shoulder.

"You too," Andre said.

"No!" Lucy exclaimed as I picked her up. "No, Brady! I want to stay with you!"

"I'll be back soon," I said.

She clung to me like a monkey. "You always say that!"

"Have I lied yet?" I hugged her back. "You stay here with Andre. The pod's no different than the alcoves. It's just like being asleep. You'll be safe here, and me and Cam and Chris will be back soon."

"Are you bringing Harry back?"

"I hope so," I told her. "That's the plan."

She loosened her grip at that, and slid into the pod with Andre. She wiped her tears as she lay down beside him. They were holding hands as the skin of the sac grew over the pod.

She'd be safe.

I had to believe that, or I never would have found the strength to step away from the pod again.

Lucy would be safe, and Doc and Andre would heal, and we were going to save Harry, and Kai-Ren would take us home again. And I decided in that moment with a kind of fierce, burning zealousness that I was going to believe those things as long as I could, until they either came true or I didn't have the anger to fight anymore.

And one thing everyone knew about me—the only thing probably—was that I was never smart enough to stop fighting.

"OKAY," Chris said once the pods were all sealed. "If the other Faceless have Harry, then we need to get him back before their ship disconnects from ours."

"And also sucks all of us into the vacuum of space," I said.

"Optimistic as always," Cam said wryly, wiping his hands on his pants. We were all covered in blood at this point. Doc's, Andre's, mine and the hybrid's. Cam's hands left dark streaks down the sides of his pants.

"The ship's injured," I said. "And there's nobody in control of her. She might not be able to seal the breach."

Chris's gaze flicked to the hybrid for a moment, and he was probably wondering the exact same thing as me. Could the hybrid control the ship? He'd got the pods activated, but could he do everything else as well? Was all Faceless technology unlocked to him? Between his Faceless DNA and our shared connection, did he hold the key to all of their tech now?

"Well, let's see what we've got then, huh?" Chris asked.

The hybrid watched Chris warily as held out a hand toward him. Then he inched forward slightly, and laid his pale hand against Chris's. Chris nodded at him, and smiled, and curled their fingers together. "You understand us, right? Not words, maybe, but *us*. You understand that we're your hive."

The hybrid has been so lonely and afraid, but there were new spikes of emotion in him now. He was cautious, but he was also curious. Maybe he didn't belong with us in the same way a newly hatched Faceless would slot right into a hive, but that was humans all over. All sharp edges and ragged feelings rubbing up against one another hard enough to cause sparks, but we made it work most of the time.

I drew a deep breath as we walked toward the exit of the pod bay, and turned around to look at the pods. Told myself again that we'd be back.

Cam stuck close as we headed up the spiraling corridor again. The ship listed heavily a few times, sending us off balance, but she was hanging in there. How much longer did we have though, before the other ship disengaged and we were blown out of the black? At the moment the other ship was both an attacker and a protector.

We hurried to the closest alcove.

"We need armor," Chris told the hybrid. "Battle armor. Do you know what I'm saying?"

The hybrid looked at us all in turn, and I felt a strange buzzing in my skull. It was pitched high, like a question, and maybe it was the hybrid trying to speak to us in turn.

"Armor," Chris repeated, and drew the hybrid into the alcove with him. "Here goes nothing, right?"

Cam and I watched as the cluster of *things* dropped from the ceiling of the alcove. They were like wet tendrils of seaweed, and they coated Chris and the hybrid in fluid as black as ink, that I knew from experience would harden into Faceless armor.

Cam put a hand on my shoulder, pulling my attention back to him. "You okay?"

"Yeah," I said, though that was probably a lie. "We've got this, right?"

"I hope so," Cam said, the corner of his mouth quirking up ruefully. "But just in case we don't get another chance to talk for a while..."

For forever, he meant.

He didn't finish that sentence. Just leaned forward and kissed me. Caught our hands together tightly, and kissed me. We were covered in sweat and blood and Faceless goo, but there was nothing gross about the kiss. I loved Cam and he loved me, and here we were again, us against the universe. Us against the *Faceless*. And in another lifetime I might have been shitting myself right now, but I still had my anger and I had something even bigger than that: Cam's love. If my anger was the storm tossed sea, then Cam's love was the rudder that kept me steady even as the wild waves drove me forward. Or maybe he was the lighthouse guiding me safely home again.

I closed my eyes briefly, and allowed myself a moment to get lost in his kiss. And then I pulled away regretfully. "I love you."

Cam rested his forehead against mine. "Love you too, Brady. Always. You're my heartbeat, remember?"

My chest ached. "And you're mine."

He straightened up, and smiled at me in that way that was ours only. It laid me bare and took my breath away at the same time because there would always be a part of me that couldn't believe I mattered to Cam. That couldn't believe I'd ever done anything in my life to deserve someone like this. And that absolutely couldn't fucking believe he felt the same way about me. And yet he showed me how wrong I was, every single day. And even if everything ended today, then at least I'd die knowing that out of everyone in the universe, Cameron Rushton loved *me*. And that was pretty fucking amazing.

A touch on my shoulder pulled my gaze away from Cam.

Chris and the hybrid loomed up behind me, features hidden in black Faceless armor that was as thin as latex but stronger than anything known to humans. It molded to their features, obscuring them entirely. I only knew it was Chris who'd tapped me on the shoulder to get my attention, because where would the hybrid have learned such a human gesture?

Chris gestured to the alcove pointedly, and Cam and I stepped inside.

I closed my eyes as the fluid began to drip down my hair and face like oil, but not before I saw Cam's grimace.

In a moment we'd be Faceless.

CHAPTER 13

AFTER A COMPLICATED SET of gestures between Chris and Cam
that was some sort of sign language for officers—or maybe they'd
taught all of us at one point and I just hadn't been paying attention—Chris took the lead. He was the one who knew his way
around Kai-Ren's ship the best. He was also the one of us most
likely to have any idea of what we were going to do once we made
it to the Stranger's ship. I hoped he did anyway, because I didn't
have a clue. So Chris took the lead, and the rest of us followed.

Everything looked different through the armor. The colors
were muted, but at the same time things looked sharper. I could
only faintly see the others' faces, and I wasn't sure how much of
that was actual sight or a whole new bunch of signals that my
brain just chose to interpret as sight.

The Faceless armor made it impossible to communicate via
speaking, so I found myself tuning in a little more to the static
buzz of our connection. There were no words there—either the
connection was too weak because Kai-Ren's hive had been deci-
mated, or the inclusion of the hybrid had scrambled the signal
somehow, but there was something there. An awareness of Cam
and Chris, I guess, and of their emotions.

The hybrid was different. His presence was a prickle down

my spine of *not right, not human, not one of us,* a sensation so deeply buried in instinct that it was impossible to parse out. The same sort of feeling my ancestors must have got, hundreds of thousands of years ago on that spinning ball of dirt, when they heard the snap of a twig behind them in the trees. That sudden jolt of fear that said *predator*—the swooping gut, the chill, the burst of fear and the rush of epinephrine that signaled danger before their conscious minds could even put it all together.

But there was something else too; a gentle but insistent prodding at the edge of my consciousness that suggested the hybrid was trying to be known to us. He was trying to connect. Trying to be a part of this human not-hive he'd found himself in. Our minds —distinct, discordant, chaotic, and linked by circumstance rather than shared purpose or biology—must have been as alien to him as he was to us.

Could he feel what was important to us? Did the lines blur, and those things became important to him as well? Did he know we were going to get Harry back from the Stranger? Did he know why Harry mattered?

There'd been a shift in me too, somewhere in the past few months, and it didn't just come from being forced to live in the other guys' heads or from having shared their memories. Harry was my friend. And yeah, I was still selfish. Guys like Cam and Chris would probably walk into hell for anyone on the same side as them—for loyalty and for duty and for that other bullshit they'd learned in officer training—and maybe they'd even do it for anyone on a different side from them, because of morality, and ethics and the sanctity of life or some bullshit. I wasn't there yet. Would never be probably, but I'd walk into hell for my friends. It wasn't like I had enough to just start tossing them aside, right?

But I liked Harry and against all odds he liked me too. No fucking way was I going to leave him to the Stranger without a fight.

Could the hybrid feel that?

Did he know the plan was to save Harry?

Though... did we even have a plan beyond that? We had

armor now, but we didn't have weapons. Maybe I'd been putting too much faith in Chris after all, because charging onto the Stranger's ship with no fucking clue what we were going to do after that sounded more like a Brady Garrett kind of plan. Probably something we should have discussed while we could still talk, right?

We moved down the corridor, the lights gleaming on our oil-slick black armor.

Diving in headfirst with no idea what we'd be facing? Definitely a Brady Garrett kind of plan.

Well, fuck it. Two decades of acting like a fucking idiot, but I was still here against all the odds. The universe hadn't killed me yet. Maybe it'd hold off a little longer after all.

There was only one way to find out.

THE STRANGER'S ship clung to ours like a fat, bloated leech. In the place it connected the walls between the ships had dissolved, or retracted, or *something*, leaving a seamless transition between his ship and ours. I might have blundered onto the Stranger's ship unknowingly, but Chris knew where the boundaries lay. He'd spend the last few months poking around in every corner he could, the curious—and faintly amused, I'd imagined sometimes, though it was probably bullshit—stares of the Faceless following him.

Chris held his hand up in warning as we crossed into the Stranger's ship.

Nothing changed as we walked deeper into the Stranger's ship except our fear. We stared down a spiral corridor that was a mirror image of the one from our ship as globs of glowing stuff slid through the walls behind us and faintly illuminated our path. There were no Faceless that we could see, and none that we could sense either. But then the Stranger's Faceless operated on a different frequency than the one we could pick up. We were going in blind.

Chris and the hybrid led the way, the hybrid tilting his head sharply every so often like a cat with twitching ears. Whatever he was listening for, it was out of our range of hearing.

We met our first Faceless half a turn down the spiral. He stood there silently, featureless black mask turned toward our approach. And he then he hissed softly, the sound like a pot boiling over and the water hitting the element.

The hybrid ignored him, and kept walking.

Hope bloomed in me. We weren't invisible, not exactly, but if we didn't read to the Faceless as a part of Kai-Ren's hive, as the enemy, then was it possible we were beneath his consideration? I'd seen it happen before with the Faceless. Back on Defender Three they'd ignored the terrified men shooting at them and walked straight through them. All our fear, our rage, our desperate need to *live*—it was nothing to the Faceless. We were nothing. The same Faceless mindset that let them swat us like mosquitoes might actually save us here.

And then the Faceless reached out suddenly, fingers closing around Chris's throat. He lifted him up, and Chris's hands clamped around the Faceless's wrist uselessly. He hung there, feet kicking, as the Faceless stared at him.

And then dropped him just as suddenly.

My heart thumped loudly as Chris scrambled to his feet, and Cam and I slipped past the Faceless.

Not quite invisible, but not enough of a threat to hold the Faceless's attention.

I sucked in a shaking breath, too afraid to break into a run, too afraid to look back. I just kept moving, one foot in front of the other, until the curve of the corridor took us out of the Faceless's sight.

The fuck was that?

I blasted the thought as loudly as any I ever had, but I didn't get an answer. Our connection was too weak. I felt more alone than I had in months, more afraid. My churning guts felt like water and my heart was racing. And then Cam reached out and squeezed my hand and I remembered that he didn't have to be in my head to read my mind.

I wondered if that Faceless, standing like a sentry close to the place where the ships were joined, was there to stop any of Kai-Ren's Faceless from coming onto their ship, or if he was there to do a headcount of the rest of his hive as they came back aboard. Was his presence there an indication that the Stranger was preparing to disengage, or was it, like everything Faceless, just fucking random and unknowable?

I thought of Harry.

I thought of Doc and Lucy and Andre, and how we had to get back to them. How we had to get them home. Because the pods might heal them, might save them and preserve them, might even shield them from an explosion if our ship was destroyed maybe, but what good was that if we couldn't get them home?

Failure, one of my instructors liked to yell at us when we were throwing ourselves through the obstacle course at basic training, *is not an option.*

Fuck that guy. What the fuck did he know about the cost of failure? What the fuck did he know about facing actual danger, and how the fuck was knowing how to climb a rope supposed to prepare me for anything like this? When we made it back to Earth I was going to look him up and visit him just to punch him in the face. And then I was going to track down every officer in the military who'd ever told me I was a useless piece of shit, and do the same to them.

And to think Doc had been worried I had no ambition.

Rationality had never been able to kill my fear but anger could, at least for a little while. It kept me on my feet now. Kept me moving forward. And that was enough.

A very human scream rang through the Stranger's ship, and we began to run. *All* of us, even the hybrid. I felt a rush of something at that. It was some tangled up emotion that I didn't have to time to unpick now, but I think in that moment a part of me decided that if Harry mattered to him too, then the hybrid was one of us.

The room we found Harry in was dark and small, and there was a strange frame protruding from the wall. Harry was hanging from it, naked, and there was a Faceless—the Stranger—standing behind him.

Fear socked me in the guts. Fear and memory, because I'd been in this exact position with Kai-Ren until Cam had stopped him. The Stranger was getting ready to envenom Harry. To force a connection so they could communicate. That's what a rational man might call it. That's what Cam had called it, because the Faceless didn't understand what rape was.

Fuck the Faceless too.

Fuck them.

The Stranger hissed and started toward us.

The hybrid lunged at him, and he couldn't be stronger than a Faceless, could he? Not with half my DNA in him.

I'd seen the Faceless fight before. They were smooth, and silent, sure of their superiority against us. And the hybrid—

My breath caught.

The hybrid fought like a scrappy fucking kid from Kopa. He didn't have the Stranger's claws. Didn't have a shred of fucking form in him, but he had anger and no sense of self-preservation. His nails, not long enough to be considered claws, were still strong enough to pierce the gloves he wore, and to shred the Stranger's mask as he tackled them both to the ground, exposing a sunken corpse-pale face. And then, like a true dirty fighter, he went straight for the Stranger's fucking eyes.

I dived onto the Stranger's legs, holding onto them tightly as the Stranger tried to thrash me off again. Above me, in a flurry of limbs, I heard hissing and spitting.

And then Chris and Cam were piling on as well.

I twisted my head just in time to see the Stranger's clawed hand slashing into my field of vision, but then someone—Chris, Cam, I couldn't tell—was gripping the Stranger tightly by the wrist and pushing his arm away.

I didn't kid myself it had anything to do with our human strength. We were like those little birds that dive-bombed attacking hawks. No way could we take the Stranger in a fair fight. Luckily the hybrid hadn't signed up for one of those.

The hybrid growled, digging his nails into the Stranger's eye socket and ripping his eye free in an explosion of thick yellow blood. And then he jabbed his fingers into the empty socket, pushing, pushing, and pushing until the Stranger fell limp underneath us, his body twitching with electrical impulses that were no longer being received in his scrambled egg brain.

Holy *shit.*

And then Chris or Cam was moving, rising to his feet and hurrying to release Harry. Cam, I thought, it was Cam. Because he was kicking at the frame and making the restraints retract the way he'd done for me. Harry fell back and Cam caught him.

"Wh—" Harry made the abortive sound a few times before he forced the question out. "What's happening?" He twisted around in Cam's hold, eyes widening as he saw the dead Stranger. "Is it—is it you guys under there? Holy fuck, please be you guys."

Cam gave him a thumbs-up. Not the human gesture I usually went with, but it did the trick.

"We need to move," I said, even though none of them could hear me. But evidentially we were all on the same page, because nobody wanted to hang around and see how the Stranger's Faceless would react now he was dead. Would it take them time to regroup, for their connection to recover, or would they come swarming? Because no fucking way would we survive a swarm. Probably wouldn't survive another single Faceless, if we were honest with ourselves.

So we moved.

WE DIDN'T STOP when we were back on our ship. Didn't even slow down. Chris caught the hybrid by the hand, and ran down the spiral corridor into the core of the ship, and we followed. We headed straight for the bridge, or at least the part of the ship we thought of as a bridge, where there were more lights, more twisting conduits and, when they'd been alive, more Faceless. I'd avoided it because of that, but Chris hadn't.

There were bodies on the floor still. I thought of the day our oxygen tanks had exploded, and the ship had sucked the debris into her walls. Was she too weak to do the same with the dead Faceless now, or was there something else that was supposed to happen to the dead? Did the Faceless have death rituals? Was there any room for that in a hive structure that had very little room for individualism?

Chris reached up behind his neck for the point that would unfasten his mask. His face was red and sweaty when he took the mask off. "Can you tell her what to do?"

The hybrid tilted his head.

I removed my own mask and stepped toward him, my fingers feeling under the back of his skull to release his mask. His face seemed less frightening now, despite what I'd just seen him do. His dark eyes were as human as mine.

"Can we disengage from the other ship?" I asked him. "And then blow those fuckers out of the black?"

The hybrid made a noise that was more like a grunt than a hiss thanks to his human larynx. And then he stepped toward one of the alcoves, his mouth pulling up at the edges in what might have been the approximation of a smile, and stepped inside.

A moment after that, the universe itself exploded.

————

THERE WERE no windows on what passed for the bridge. There was no way for us to know what was happening outside, but it felt as though we were a leaf caught in a maelstrom, churned on the boiling water, sucked under and dumped over and over again. I ended up on the floor, my fingers scrabbling uselessly in the slime for purchase, as the ship rolled and dived.

And then as abruptly as it began it was over, and I was wedged against Chris at the base of an alcove, staring at the dark ceiling and sucking in a series of shaky breaths that didn't seem to fill my lungs at all. I blinked as the lights in the walls settled into their regular pulsing rhythm again instead of bouncing around like fireflies in a bottle.

"The fuck just happened?" Harry rasped from somewhere nearby.

Cam loomed over me, reaching down to help me to my feet. "Are we okay? I think we're okay."

Chris scrambled up. "A window. We need a window."

The three of us followed him to the closest window.

My stomach dropped as I stared out into the nebula.

Backlit against a shining green cloud and receding rapidly into the distance as we moved, a Faceless ship burned. It could only be the Stranger's ship. It spun slowly, bleeding gas or fluid into space. It's exterior, usually black and formless, was illuminated by a series of explosions that shuddered through it. The explosions tore through the ship, and then along the trailing threads of gas or fluid only to be immediately quenched again by the vacuum of space.

There was a cluster of other Faceless ships dotted black against the shifting clouds of the nebula, but none appeared to be following us.

"Holy shit," Chris said. "Did we just *win?*"

A startled laugh burst of out me, because how crazy was that? Okay, so we were clearly in full-on retreat mode, but we were alive and none of the other Faceless were chasing us, and that sure as shit counted as a win in my book. Well, almost.

I peeled away from the others, and hurried toward the pod bay. I'd hardly taken a few steps before I realized the others were following. All except for Chris.

"I'm going back to the bridge," he called.

Of course he was. Because that was Chris all over. He needed to be where the action was. He needed to know exactly what was going on with the ship and with the hybrid.

Cam and Harry and I headed for the pod bay. My heart was in my mouth by the time I reached it because I didn't trust the universe not to fuck me over in some way. I reached Doc's pod first because I couldn't bring myself to look into Lucy's without any forewarning. I stared down at Doc as he lay suspended in milky fluid. His shirt, pulled open during Cam's attempts at CPR, floated around him, buoyed by the unseen current that pulsed through the pod. His hairy chest and stomach appeared uninjured, but I couldn't tell if he was breathing or not.

I drew a breath, and pressed my hand to the sac of the pod. Like magic, Doc's hand rose to meet mine. I could feel the calluses on his palm through the thin skin of the sac. A series of glowing characters appeared across his belly.

We'd fucked this up so badly once, with Cam. We hadn't known how to get him out of the pod and we'd made a mess of it and almost killed Cam in the process. But now I knew. I pressed my other hand to the skin of the pod, and Doc lifted his.

The illuminated characters flickered and disappeared, and then the skin of the pod began to melt away, drawing back to the edges of the carapace. The fluid in the pod drained slowly away until Doc lay in the bottom of the pod.

He coughed suddenly, spraying me with fluid, and his eyes opened.

"Okay," I said as I wiped his spit and whatever the fuck else it was off my face. "You're okay." I helped pull him into a sitting position so he could clear his lungs more easily. "Shit, you're okay."

Doc blinked at me dozily for a moment, and then stared down at his unmarked skin. "Jesus. What the hell just happened?"

"We're not dead," I said, "and the hybrid is flying the ship."

Doc blinked again. "Well, fuck me."

Which pretty much summed it up, I guess.

WE WERE A STRANGELY fragile group who assembled that night for our regular scheduled debrief. Harry was quiet and jumpy, trying too hard to pretend he wasn't freaked out by what had happened. The Stranger hadn't raped him, but that didn't mean the violation didn't count. It counted, and it'd take Harry a while to come to terms with that. Andre and Doc had their own shit to deal with, after they'd both thought they were dead men. Lucy was quiet too, sticking close to me and Cam and shooting curious glances at the hybrid, like she didn't know if he was terrifying after hearing what he'd done, or wanting to befriend him like he was a stray cat.

"As far as I can tell, we're going home," Chris said.

The hybrid mouthed the word curiously: *Home.*

"We found four Faceless survivors," Chris continued. "We've put them in the pods."

"And we're keeping them there?" Harry asked suddenly, chewing the skin at the side of his thumbnail. "With Kai-Ren?"

Chris nodded. "Unless we need them for something, yeah."

I felt a burn of satisfaction in my gut at that. Because why let Kai-Ren out now, when we could do this without him? Fuck him and fuck the Faceless. We were in charge for once, and we were done with being his puppets or his pets or whatever the fuck he thought we were. We'd saved his life and his ship. We didn't owe him anything more than that. We didn't owe him our worship just for being stronger than us.

Andre shifted on his bunk, the canvas creaking under him. "And we're not being followed?"

"No sign of it, no," Chris said.

Andre nodded, but his brow was furrowed. "Because what if we just started a Faceless civil war?" he asked. "What does that mean for us?"

Chris shrugged. "Maybe if they're busy killing each other, they'll keep their eyes off us for a while."

I studied him closely for a moment, feeling the faintest residual hint of sharp satisfaction rolling off him. And I remembered, suddenly, what Doc had said weeks ago now: *"What are the chances those boys from intel aren't already ten steps ahead of me?"* Because somehow everything had come up roses for Chris, hadn't it? And he couldn't have planned it—nobody could have—but through the hybrid we'd gained control of a Faceless ship, we'd killed a Faceless in actual hand-to-hand combat, and blown another Faceless ship out of the sky. Chris had come looking for all the secrets of Faceless technology, and he didn't have them yet, not exactly, but he had the key to them: the hybrid.

And right then I didn't give a fuck what Chris was planning, what game he was playing, or how far ahead he was thinking. The people I loved were alive and we were going home. That was all that mattered to me, and that's all that had ever mattered. In the beginning, it had only been my dad and Lucy that I'd cared about, but then there was Doc, and then Cam, and now there were more people on that short list than someone like me deserved. But I'd take it.

The debrief wound down a little after that. I was tired and hungry, but not hungry enough to go into an alcove. I wanted to stick close to Lucy just as much as she was sticking close to me, so I shook out my damp blanket and crawled under it. I held up the edge so Lucy got the invitation, and she squirmed in beside me. There wasn't really enough room for Cam as well, but we made it work. I'd never sleep like this, with Lucy's knee digging into my stomach and Cam wedged in behind me. Didn't matter though, because this was perfect.

I closed my eyes and listened to the sounds of the others getting ready for bed: Andre and Harry talking in low voices, Doc scratchily clearing his throat, the creak of canvas, Chris saying something to the hybrid and the hybrid answering with a questioning hum.

We were alive.

I smiled, and warmth burst in my chest.

We were alive and going home.

CHAPTER 14

THE NEXT DAY brought us close to what must have been the edge of the nebula. The clouds were wisps now, and starlight blinked behind them. I never thought I'd be looking forward to being in the black again. I stretched as I peered out the window, and then dug through my footlocker for clothes that weren't totally gross. Everything was pretty much covered in the residual slime that covered the Faceless ship, but I wanted something that wasn't stained with blood, either Doc and Andre's, or the gross yellow stuff from the Stranger which was smeared like ochre across my pants.

I wasn't awake late, but Chris had already been up for hours—of course—and had drawn up a list of duties for every single one of us in one of his notebooks.

"This is why you broke up with him, right?" I asked Cam as Chris outlined our new roster to us. "He's fucking insufferable."

"Want me to write you up for insubordination, Crewman Garrett?" Chris asked. His brows were arched in a challenge, but there was a smile fighting to be known in the twitch of his mouth.

"Want me to tell you to go fuck yourself?"

"Swear jar!" Lucy said, but didn't bother cup her hands. She knew we'd run out of shit to give her.

Cam rolled his eyes at the pair of us.

Despite Chris's need to impose order on our comfortable chaos, he actually had some good ideas. We'd do rounds now, walking through every part of the Faceless ship we could and reporting any damage—or whatever we thought looked like damage—to Chris. Rounds also included checking out all the windows to make sure we weren't being followed. I had no idea how useful our human eyesight would be out here, but it was slightly better than the Faceless taking us totally by surprise.

Doc and I were also in charge of monitoring the pods by virtue of our medical training, even though nothing in that remotely qualified us to know if Kai-Ren and his surviving Faceless were actually doing okay in there or not. Nobody else was given any extra duties, but what was there to do except to monitor our situation and hope it didn't suddenly go sideways? Same as fucking always.

It was weird though. Our new routine—constantly walking the ship and reporting to Chris down on the bridge—gave us more purpose than we'd had in months. We weren't just passengers anymore. And it kept us busy enough that our breaks felt well earned. Didn't stop me from bitching about it though.

"If I have to walk up this corridor one more fucking time," I groaned, and threw myself down on the cot in Doc's medbay.

"There's nothing for it, son," Doc said mildly, looking up from whatever book he was reading. "We'll have to mutiny."

"Fuck off," I told him with a grin. "Don't even joke about that. You know I would."

Doc grinned right back at me, and set his book aside so we could go and inspect the pods for the third time that day.

That little wind-up clock was ruling our lives more than ever, but I didn't really mind. Time might have been arbitrary out here where it got mixed up with speed and distance and turned into some mind-bending bullshit I could never understand, but each little tick of that little clock brought us closer to home.

We weren't the only ones inspecting the pods. Chris was leaning over one, one hand pressed to the skin of the sac to make the glowing characters light up, and holding himself twisted up like a pretzel with his notebook against his raised knee while he tried to copy the figures down. The hybrid was watching him curiously.

"Aren't you supposed to be driving this thing?" I asked him as Doc and I approached.

Chris straightened up, catching his notebook before he dropped it. He tucked it into a pocket on the thigh of his pants. "She's alive, and she knows where she's going. Thomas doesn't need to do anything except check in every now and then."

"Thomas?" I asked, and the hybrid looked over to me at the sound of his name. "You gave that to him?"

"He wanted a name," Chris said. "We all have names."

I searched through my catalogue of Chris's memories, but I'd never heard him think of a Thomas. No family, no friend, no ex. "I thought you'd go for something more obvious like Adam. First of a new species and all that."

Chris shrugged. "It is kind of obvious. It means 'twin'."

The jolt that went through me was a little unsettling. It was weird enough looking at the hybrid and seeing a face that was a strange amalgam of mine and a Faceless's, and I'd been trying to think of him as an individual since he'd helped us get Harry back. The reminder that he shared half my DNA wasn't a welcome one. But it also wasn't his fault.

"Thomas," I said, and the hybrid looked at me again. "You like that name?"

"Thomas," he said back to me, stumbling clumsily over the word. A spoken word, not one reliant on any Faceless connection. A *real* word that any other human would have been able to hear.

"Holy shit," I said. "You can *speak?*"

Thomas hissed proudly, and then blinked at Doc as Doc bustled toward him for a quick inspection of his mouth and tongue. If he'd seen how dangerous Thomas was, he might have been a little less eager to put his fingers in his mouth, but Thomas underwent his examination placidly enough.

I crossed over to the pod, and stared down at Kai-Ren. "You

want to draw the characters?" I asked Chris. "I'll keep my hand here while you do."

"Thanks," Chris said, and fished his notebook out of his pocket again.

I pressed my hand down on the sac gently, and Kai-Ren's gloved hand lifted to meet mine. Moments later, the inside of the pod lit up with the glowing characters it projected across his oily black battle armor. I wondered if it said anything different than it did when we were in there. That's what Chris was wondering too, probably, and why he was here doing this. This was just the start, I was sure, of his fevered attempt to record absolutely everything he could while we were still onboard.

I looked away from Kai-Ren, and watched Chris work instead. "You really think any of this will be useful once we get home?"

"I don't know." Chris chewed the inside of his cheek for a moment, and glanced over at Thomas. His expression clouded. "I have no idea what's going to happen when we get home."

ON THE THIRD day after the battle we left the nebula completely behind. The clouds slipped away slowly, and then we were surrounded by starlight again. The temperature inside the ship dropped enough that I dug through my footlocker for another shirt to pull on and then I sat on my cot, wishing I had a cigarette, and watched the stars slide by in our slipstream. It was the middle of the day according to Doc's wind-up clock, and I was alone in the room. Thomas was driving this thing and Chris was probably hovering over his shoulder while he did it. Harry and Andre were doing another inventory of our remaining supplies, or lack thereof —fuck knows why—and last I'd seen Lucy was helping them out by ticking things off on a checklist of her own devising. She'd probably run the military one day with the head start she was getting now in pointless fucking bureaucracy. And Doc was sneaking a nap in the medbay.

It was alone as things got on the ship, so when I looked over and saw Cam leaning in the doorway for a second I was torn between admiring the definition of his biceps while he stood there in a gray singlet with his arms crossed, and beckoning him closer. I went with the second option, always greedy to touch him.

He sat down on the cot beside me.

"Nah," I said, and lay down. "Come here."

I shifted my legs apart so he could lie in the cradle of my thighs and then lifted my face for a kiss.

"Brady," he said, huffing out a warm breath of surprise. "It's the middle of the day."

"Dark as fucking midnight outside."

"Smartass." He pinched me on the hip for that. "But anyone could walk in."

"Probably won't though."

"You can't know that." But he dipped his head down and kissed me again, his tongue sliding against mine briefly.

I arched against him, making sure he could feel my hardening dick. "When was the last time we fucked in a bed?"

"Made love," he corrected me.

"Whatever." I got a hand between us, tugging the button on his pants free. "When was the last time?"

"Defender Three." He bucked against me as I got a hand in his pants and went straight for his dick. "Last time we were there."

Had we? I could remember fucking up against the bathroom mirror pretty clearly. Yeah, we'd probably done it in a bed there as well, just like we had the first time the brass had stuck us in a room together.

"Come on," I urged him. "I wanna do it in a bed again."

Cam stilled for a moment, and held my gaze like he was searching for something. "You mean you want to do it now, while Kai-Ren's still in a pod."

Could never hide a fucking thing from him, the asshole. The dumb thing was I hadn't even known that was the reason until he'd said it.

"Yeah." I exhaled heavily. "I want to do it without having to look over my shoulder and see him standing there."

Or touching.

Which...sometimes it felt good. Strange or powerful or something in ways I didn't want to think about too deeply. But sometimes I just wanted it to be me and Cam, and with the surviving Faceless in the pods the connection was the weakest it had been in months. Apart from Cam's freaky prescience, of course, but I think that was all him. Or I was as easy to read as a book. The sort with pictures that popped up.

Cam leaned down and kissed me again.

It took us a little while to find our heat again—making love was a little slower than fucking, it turned out—but it wasn't long before we were both trying not to elbow each other in the face or kick each other in the balls as we shucked our shirts and pants off. And then we were skin on skin, soft kisses and heated breath, and our bodies moving together in ways that were both familiar and new, every time.

"Want you to top," I whispered to him. "But face to face."

"Yeah," he breathed back to me. "I want that too."

Cam lifted off me briefly, stretching to reach the wall and coat his hand in the viscous goo that the ship produced. Which, yeah, gross, but we'd both learned pretty early on to push it to the backs of our minds. Everything here was so fucking gross really. First thing I had planned for when I got home was a shower hot enough to take off at least three layers of skin.

I pulled my legs up and spread my knees, and Cam knelt on the cot. His dick was hard and shining with the fluid, and I wanted it in me.

"Hold on," he said. "Can you..."

He took me by the hands and we sort of shifted around until he got me where he wanted me—straddling his thighs, my arms around his neck. And then he held me open as I lowered myself onto his dick. It stung at first, the angle tight and weird, but then Cam shifted and everything fell into place. We slid into a slow rhythm, gentle as the rocking of the waves, and Cam lifted his face so that we could kiss at the same time.

"I love you," I said, because I never got tired of saying it and hearing him say it back to me.

"Love you," he echoed, his fingers tightening on my hips. "I love you so much."

I sucked in a breath as our pace picked up, and we went from moving slowly to both pushing for the finish line. I closed my eyes and dropped my head back, chasing all the pleasure Cam could give me. I shivered when he licked a line up my exposed throat, and my balls tightened. My dick was hard and throbbing between us, and it didn't take much at all to push me over the edge.

It never did.

I came, jerking and shuddering in Cam's grasp, and pulling him over the edge with me.

We came down by degrees, with slow kisses and whispered words, hearts beating together.

And then, just to piss on our afterglow, Doc said from the door, "Could you at least pin up a blanket? You two aren't the only ones who have to live here, you know? Jesus Christ!"

Cam flushed, bright red, and I gave Doc the finger. Cam turned his face into my throat and laughed, hot gusts of his breath cooling my sweat-slick skin as his body shook.

LUCY MIGHT HAVE THOUGHT Thomas was just a baby when I'd cut him in the pod bay after everything went to shit with the Stranger, but in the space of a few days his language came along in leaps and bounds. He was part of our small hive. He knew what we knew. He didn't have to learn from scratch like a human child. The knowledge was already there. It was just a matter of unlocking it. He listened avidly to our conversations, prompting us with curious sounds to continue talking. He was fascinated by Doc's collection of books, though written language was still out of his grasp for now, and just as fascinated by our clothes. He started to wear pants and a shirt because that's what we did. And he started drawing with Lucy, making small disgruntled noises when his pictures didn't turn out like he wanted. He drew humanoid figures, and his dark eyes widened in fascination whenever Lucy drew a fish, or a cow, or a dog and told him all about the petting zoo I'd promised to take her to when we made it home.

I wasn't the only one who watched Thomas with a worried frown on my face.

"The thing is," I said to Harry as he joined me for rounds one afternoon, "you know what you assholes in intel did to me and Cam back home, right?"

Harry winced. "Yeah."

A glass cell in an underground room. They'd ripped us from our lives, from Lucy, and put us in total isolation against every rule in the book because they thought the Faceless were communicating with us again. Which turned out they were, but that didn't mean we were traitors colluding with the enemy or any bullshit like that. We didn't have any control over it.

"Well what do you think they're gonna do to Thomas?" I asked, dodging around something that in a regular ship might have been called a conduit, but here looked more like a pulsing vein. "You think they're gonna let him out for days at the petting zoo?"

Harry's nose wrinkled. "Why would he want to go to a petting zoo?"

Harry must have missed that conversation with Lucy.

"Trust me," I said, "he does. It's his fucking life's ambition right now to hold a baby goat. Or it was yesterday. He might have moved on to quantum physics by now. But my point is, he's going to be locked up in some cage, isn't he? And he's going to be taken apart by our scientists, over and over again until there's nothing left of him, and that's not fair."

"Yeah, I know." Harry chewed his bottom lip for a moment. "But it's not like we can leave him with the Faceless, is it?"

I thought of how Kai-Ren had killed the other hatchlings. Leaving Thomas with him might even be a mercy. At least it would be over quickly, however much the thought of it made my guts churn.

"I guess not," I said, but the thought of what would happen to Thomas continued to bite at me.

He'd saved us. More than that, he was one of us, wasn't he? He'd decided that our weird little group of humans was his hive. And maybe it was the DNA he shared with me that had stuck him with us to begin with, but now he was drawing pictures and learning to talk and figuring out how to smile when we did. He was teaching himself how to be human, not Faceless. And he'd never learn that in an underground cage.

I took my concerns to Doc, to Cam, to Harry and to Andre. And then, when I couldn't drag my feet about it any more, I took them to Chris.

I found him at the bridge, like always, taking copious notes, like always. I looked around for Thomas, and saw that he was in one of the alcoves, the translucent walls closed around him as he did whatever the fuck it was he did to keep the ship going in the right direction.

"Hey," I said awkwardly.

Chris looked up from his notebook. "Hey. What's up?"

I swiped my tongue over my lower lip. "What's going to happen to Thomas when we get home?"

Chris regarded me steadily. "I don't know."

"Yeah, I figured," I said. "And that's not good enough. You gonna stand by and let them take him away? He's a *person*." I shrugged. "Well, close enough."

"I'm not going to let anyone hurt him," Chris said.

"Fuck off with that!" I rolled my eyes. "How are you going to stop it from happening? You can tell yourself something like that a million times, until you're blue in the face. You can even *believe* it, but it doesn't mean shit, because when it comes down to it, when some asshole who's bigger than you gets in your way, there's *nothing* you can do to stop it!"

Chris didn't get it. He hadn't spent his whole life kicking against walls and getting fucking nowhere. He hadn't been shut down constantly by arbitrary rules enforced by assholes who just didn't give a fuck. The rules had never fucked Chris over because he'd never had to push back against them. Why would he? The rules were made by guys like him for guys like him. He'd never felt helpless because he'd never been helpless. But he would be. This time, he would be, because there was no way the military wouldn't take Thomas away.

I clenched my fists, wanting to throw a punch, but not at him. At *everything*. Story of my life.

"Brady." Chris took a step toward me, tucking his notebook into his pocket.

I glared.

"Hey." He put his hand on my shoulders, jostling me so that I was facing him. His expression was open, earnest. His eyes were dark in the gloom of the bridge, but I remembered them from all the times I'd seen them in Cam's dreams: a blue as deep as the sea when a sudden ledge dropped away underneath you. "Brady, I'm not going to let anything happen to Thomas, okay? I'm not."

I shook my head. "It's not your choice though!"

His mouth quirked. "Have you ever won a game of poker on a really shitty hand?"

"Yeah. Sometimes. So?"

"How'd you do it?" he asked me.

"I dunno. I bluffed."

Chris grinned and released me. "Yeah, you bluffed."

What the fuck did that mean?

He laughed at the look on my face. "Jesus. Brady, we just survived a battle with the Faceless, and you think we can't protect Thomas? We've got this, okay? We've got this."

Lack of confidence had never been Chris's problem. And as much as I wanted to believe him, optimism had never been one of my strengths.

"We've got this," he said again, his voice softening.

"Yeah," I said, even though I didn't believe it for a second, because the universe always found some new and exciting way to shit all over me. "Okay."

And then I turned and left before I couldn't hold back that urge to punch something.

THERE WAS a place at the edge of the universe where speed and mass collided and did weird shit with time. It was way beyond my fucking understanding, but what was new about that? Whatever the reason was, the days started to drag on longer and longer the closer we got to home, even with all our new duties filling them. I tried to explain it to Cam, that feeling like time itself had slowed, and he laughed at me, the fucker.

"It has nothing to do with relativity, Brady," he told me. "This is like December."

"What?"

"When I was a kid," he said, making some mark in his notebook as we walked along the glowing corridors of the ship, "the longest month in the world was December. My parents put the tree up on the first, and I had a little advent calendar and everything, and I was looking forward to Christmas Day so much that it took *forever*. I wanted my presents so badly!" He laughed at the memory. "December was so slow, but January? With school right around the corner? That flew right past."

The only thing I'd ever counted down was how many years, months and days I had left in my military service. I'd done it first just trying to make the numbers work for me—would Dad live long enough to support Lucy until I could get home?—but they never did add up right.

My chest ached. I wished Dad had known that Lucy was safe. I wished he hadn't died thinking I'd failed. He must have been so scared for her at the end.

"Hey," Cam caught my hand. "You okay? We can do Christmas when we're home. With a tree and presents for you and Lucy."

"Yeah, I don't care about Christmas." I swallowed around the lump in my throat. "I was thinking about Dad. About how he didn't know Lucy would be okay."

Cam, to his credit, didn't offer me any bullshit platitudes. He just pulled me into a hug. "I'm sorry."

"I'm just being dumb for no reason," I said, leaning my head on his shoulder. "Just...whenever things are going right, I have to start thinking of all the bad stuff or something, I don't know."

"That's okay," Cam said. He ran a hand down my back. "Because guess what, Brady?"

I straightened up so I could look him in the eye. "What?"

"You've got a whole lifetime in front of you to figure out that getting something good doesn't mean something bad is just around the corner." He leaned in and pressed our foreheads together. "And I'm gonna be there with you all the way, giving you as many good days as I can."

I wrinkled my nose. "That's not fair."

"No," he said, shaking his head slightly. "It is fair, Brady, because you make all of my days better just by being in them."

"Even when I'm being an asshole?"

Cam smiled. "I knew what I was signing up for."

I huffed out a laugh at that. "Oh, no rebuttal on the asshole thing? I'm not the only one in this relationship, I guess."

"You're really not," Cam agreed. His smile faded. "I told myself I missed the starlight. I told myself my fear at coming back onboard this ship was irrational. I told myself that what Kai-Ren did to me didn't matter. And I told everyone else that too. And you're the only one who called bullshit on that. You're the only one who knew I was lying."

I laid my hand against his cheek.

"I think, when this is done," he said, his voice so soft I had to strain to hear him, "that I'll do all my stargazing from our balcony."

"Yeah," I breathed. "That sounds like a good plan."

Home.

We were going home.

CHAPTER 15

THE DEFENDER HUNG IN SPACE, a speck of gray against the black. It seemed so tiny and inconsequential. It seemed peaceful too but the moment our ship had appeared, blocking out the stars, the guys on board must have been frantic with activity, like ants in a jar that had just been shaken up. And then the Hawks came, buzzing past us like insects. They weren't firing though. Maybe they were honoring the treaty with Kai-Ren, even though they couldn't have known this was his ship. We'd taken radios with us when we left, but the batteries had long since corroded. Andre had tried for hours to get one working again, and in the end he'd just tossed it aside and said, "Fuck this."

So the Hawks weren't firing. Maybe because of the treaty, and maybe because they knew from experience that an attack on a Faceless ship was a suicide run. Years ago now, a formation of Hawks had seen off a Faceless ship. Knowing what I knew about the Faceless now, I wondered if they'd just got bored and left. Or maybe it had never happened like that at all, but someone in the military had decided that we all needed the morale boost of believing that it had. I thought of the poster of Cam's face, and the footage of his capture that was never shown in its entirety on Earth.

Jesus fuck, I hated the Defenders and the military and everything they stood for, but I didn't even have the words for the sheer amount of happiness that bubbled up inside me as we drew closer to that rusty tin can spinning slowly in the black.

The guys on the Defender weren't the only ones as busy as ants. I had shit strewn all over the floor of our room that I had to pack into my footlocker, and so did Lucy. She was just a kid. I didn't have that excuse. I threw everything in, not even caring to check if it was mine, and left Lucy sorting through her drawings—why, I have no idea since all she needed to do was put them in her footlocker—and went and helped Doc start packing up his medical bay. It was his books mainly, their pages soft and fragile with the moisture they'd sucked up from the air around us.

"I never really thought this would happen," I admitted as I stacked a bunch of books in a plastic crate.

Doc threw me a sidelong look, his caterpillar eyebrows tugging together. "And you think you're the only one?"

I considered that for a moment. "I suppose not. Hey, they're not going to shoot us out of the sky before we get to them, are they?"

Doc snorted. "Not unless we've made leaps and bounds in weapons technology in the past couple of months, they're not. Now stop worrying and get packing."

I grinned. "Sounds like a plan, Doc."

It took another hour or so to reach the Defender, Doc's wind-up clock counting down every painstaking minute.

"Okay," Chris said, when the Defender was looming up close enough that we could make out the tubes on the Outer Ring. "When we dock, they're going to be on high alert. So I'll go out first, and I want everyone to stay back. Thomas especially."

If Chris was volunteering to be the guy shot by a nervous marine, that was fine with me.

"We carry our own stuff off," Chris said. "We don't let them aboard."

"Why?" I asked.

"Because we've got five Faceless in the pods who, at the

moment, are entirely at our mercy," Chris said. "And we don't need the brass to know that and make some decision that will fuck everything up for everyone."

He glanced at Thomas when he said it.

"What's your angle?" Harry asked, lifting his chin.

"I'm still working on it," Chris said. "I just need you guys to back me up."

Harry nodded. "Yeah. Of course."

When we'd left months ago, we'd been guys in uniform with military haircuts and—for the rest of them, anyway—at least a nominal respect for the command structure. And now I couldn't remember the last time I'd heard anyone use rank, let alone seriously try to pull it on someone else. The military weren't going to recognize the scruffy barefoot assholes about to walk through the walls of their Defender. I kind of liked them though. Turns out they were my sort of assholes.

The Faceless ship hit the Defender like jelly. There was no real impact, and if there was we didn't feel it. The ship didn't crash into the Defender—it yielded to it, and then clung like a limpet. The stench of burning metal drew us to one of the higher decks of the ship and we reached it just in time to see the Faceless ship's skin opening.

A blast of dry air hit us, and it felt so fucking *good*.

Behind that blast I saw the gray metal walls of the Defender. Echoing through them, above the sound of a wailing klaxon, I could hear boots ringing on the floor. I grinned and held Lucy's hand tightly.

The boots stopped—guys getting into position. Chris gave them a moment to get a handle on their nerves, and then stepped into the breached wall.

"My name is Captain Chris Varro," he called in a loud, clear voice. "Place your weapons down, please. You're not under attack."

There was a moment of silence, then harsh, whispered conversation, and then a man wearing a marine's insignia walked into view. "Captain Varro?" He gave a salute. "Welcome to Defender Three, sir."

I exchanged a wide-eyed look with Cam, and almost choked on a laugh.

What were the fucking odds?

CHRIS WAS serious as hell about not allowing any Defender personnel onto the Faceless ship. He was also a good liar.

"Not my rules, Commander Leonski," he said to my former C.O. as soon as the guy appeared. "Battle Regent Kai-Ren has been very clear on the protocols."

I exchanged a look with Cam as we walked after them.

Our grubby little party was flanked by marines. Their boots rang on the metal floors. Our bare feet squelched and squeaked as we trailed Faceless goo behind us. What a fucking sight we must have been. We were scruffy-haired, our damp haphazard uniforms stuck to us, and the stench rolling off us was no small thing either. We'd grown immune to it on our months onboard the Faceless ship, but nothing inside that ship had exactly smelled of roses. It was way too biological for that.

Thomas, walking behind Chris, was twitchy. He didn't need to be connected to these guys to smell the fear and hostility coming off them. We should have made him wear Faceless armor, I thought. Might have been better to leave his face up to their imaginations. Thomas was never gonna win any beauty pageants on Earth, was he? That made two of us, I guess.

We were escorted from the Outer Ring to the Inner Ring, which was mostly made up of sleeping quarters and rec facilities. The Outer Ring was for docking, the Inner Ring was for personnel, and the Core was for the real business of the station. Ops, the medbay, the Dome, administration, and underneath everything else the reactor that kept the Defender running. We didn't stop in the Inner Ring, of course, because Commander Leonski's priorities didn't include getting us showers. We blew right though it and headed for the Core of Defender Three.

It was there, in a bland gray-walled conference room, that Chris made his play. And what a hell of a play it was. It was simple and at the same time breathtakingly audacious.

"This is Thomas," Chris said, staring Leonski right in the eye. "He is the chosen ambassador of the Faceless battle regent Kai-Ren."

And just like that Thomas was saved a lifetime of captivity getting poked and prodded by scientists. If the military thought he had Kai-Ren's protection, they wouldn't dare touch a hair on his weird hybrid head. And with Kai-Ren safely tucked away in stasis, who was going to tell them that the Faceless thought Thomas was an abomination? Who was going to tell them what had happened to the other hatchlings?

The rest was anticlimactic. Doc shook Leonski's hand, clapped him on the back like they were old friends—they were, I guess—and told everyone in the room exactly how many people he'd be willing to kill for a shower, a clean uniform, cigarettes and food. A little while after that we were in the officer's rec lounge, clean and pink and dry, sitting around a large table and watching Thomas poking curiously at a bowl of oatmeal. Because as much as we all wanted to rip into steaks, Doc had decided that after months on a liquid diet we needed to pace ourselves. The oatmeal was good, so I didn't even complain much, especially when I got a soda for the first time in months, and the bubbles and the sugar rush almost made me come right then and there.

"So," Doc said, lowering his voice so that the marines by the door couldn't hear us. "Chosen ambassador of the battle regent Kai-Ren, huh?"

"Yeah." Chris glanced at Cam, and his mouth quirked. "Turns out there really isn't a good way to explain the unexplainable to the military. So you fudge the translations a little."

Fudge the translations? Kai-Ren had literally torn Thomas's fellow hatchlings apart. Cam had fudged the translations when he'd described Kai-Ren as a battle regent. Chris had blatantly fucking lied. And fucking good on him for doing it as well. There wasn't a lot of space to maneuver between the Faceless and the military, but Chris had found it and exploited it.

"Hey, don't blame me," Chris said in response to my snort. "Cam started it with all his battle regent bullshit."

Cam raised his brows. "Pardon me for trying to save the human race."

Chris nodded. "I get it now. I didn't then, but I get it now."

He glanced at Thomas, and Thomas made a humming sound as he spooned some oatmeal into his mouth.

"Good?" Chris asked, the skin around his eyes crinkling when he smiled.

"Good," Thomas echoed around his oatmeal, his throat working furiously as he figured out how to swallow something with more substance than Faceless goo.

Lucy leaned into my side, and I put an arm around her shoulders. All of the clothes that had been made for her before we'd started our journey with the Faceless were still onboard the ship, so she was wearing a clean T-shirt as a dress, and kept hitching up the smallest pair of boxer briefs the Q-store carried. The military didn't really cater for eight-year-old girls. Her hair hung in wet little twists down her back, darkening the gray fabric of the T-shirt. Now that her belly was full for the first time in months, she was blinking slowly and clearly fighting sleep. I knew how she felt. I wanted nothing more than to be given a decent fucking bed in the officers' quarters—the benefits of Cam's rank rather than mine—and to curl up under the blankets and sleep for hours with Cam on one side of me and Lucy on the other. My feet weren't in the red dirt yet, but I could go there in my dreams.

Except we couldn't sleep just yet.

There were still things we had to do.

We finished our food, and Doc went and enquired about quarters. He offered to stay with Thomas and Lucy in whatever accommodations could be found for them while the rest of us went and cleared out our belongings from the Faceless ship. He just didn't want to lift those boxes of books himself, probably. But I squeezed his shoulder in thanks as I passed him.

It was weird, walking in boots again after so long. Weird wearing clothes that weren't damp. The air on Defender Three felt too dry and too sharp, and I wasn't the only one who cleared his scratchy throat and coughed as we made our way back to the Faceless ship with our marine escort following.

It was weird leaving the straight gray walls of the Defender, the rusted rivets and the seams of metal, and stepping into the Faceless ship again where everything was darker and damper and stranger. Where everything, however much we'd gotten used to it over the past months, suddenly felt starkly alien all over again.

I'd been right when I'd told Cam I wasn't made for this. I dragged my fingers along a glowing wall and watched as it bowed under the slight pressure. A little more and I knew it would open up and let me slip inside like it had before. And it turned out that maybe I didn't just need solid ground underneath my feet. Turned out I needed fucking walls to be walls as well.

The ship no longer scared me, but I didn't belong here. None of us did.

Andre and Harry headed for our room to get a start on unloading our gear, and Chris and Cam and I made our way down the spiral toward the pod bay.

The pods gleamed, and I remembered the first time I'd seen one. Like a rhinoceros beetle laying on its back, I'd thought then, with its legs hugging the sac. The strangeness of it, and the fear, had faded while I'd been onboard, but something about my clean uniform and my dry skin and the fact that the smooth grey metal walls of Defender Three were right outside was reigniting that old fear all over again. Everything here was so alien. How had I forgotten that, even for a minute?

"You ready?" Chris asked, but he didn't move any closer to the pods.

Cam nodded, and stepped forward.

"I'll do it," I said, my heart thumping. The way Cam brought himself up so quickly told me that I'd made the right choice.

I approached the first pod, and lifted myself up onto my toes to stare down past the skin of the sac and into the milky fluid. Kai-Ren floated there, the gash in his mask exposing the white skin of his skull-like face and his closed eyes.

I raised my hand and placed it on the sac. Kai-Ren's gloved hand came up and rested on mine. The skin of the sac slid between our hands. I drew a deep breath, and put my other hand on the sac. And Kai-Ren touched it, completing the circuit, and the skin of the sac began to dissolve as the fluid inside drained away.

Kai-Ren sucked in a wet breath, and opened his yellow eyes. His gaze held mine. "Bray-dee. Little one."

There was a strange buzzing in my ears like tinnitus. The connection was faltering, I realized. It was skipping channels like a busted old radio looking for a good signal. Kai-Ren wasn't strong anymore. With his hive mostly destroyed and with the four other survivors still in stasis, the connection was the weakest it had ever been.

Didn't mean he couldn't snap our necks without breaking a sweat though.

I stepped back from the pod as he climbed out of it. I'd almost forgotten how tall he was, how terrifying. And now, with his mask hanging like torn skin from his death's head face, he looked like the creature from every nightmare I'd ever had again.

My breath caught in my throat, and Cam put his hand on my lower back.

Kai-Ren stared narrowly between us.

"We are at Defender Three," Chris said. "There is only you and four other survivors left from your hive. We saved your ship. We have repaid your hospitality, and you're going to leave now, and never come back."

I'd liked Chris's audacity when he used it with Leonski. Here, it terrified me.

Chris lifted his chin. "You're going to honor the treaty, and swear that the other hives will too."

I couldn't have been the only one wondering how much control Kai-Ren had over the other hives right now. Then again, we'd technically won the battle with the Stranger, right? Maybe that would give him time enough to build up his hive again. And maybe I didn't give a fuck, as long as he was gone.

Kai-Ren narrowed his eyes at Chris. "You make demands of me? You are *nothing.*"

Chris didn't even flinch. He might have even smiled. "If we were nothing, you would be dead."

Kai-Ren snarled. "How are you alive?"

This time there was no mistaking Chris's smile. "We destroyed the other Faceless ship."

Kai-Ren hissed at that, because of course he knew how we'd done it. There was only one possibility. He curled his thin lips back, sharp teeth gleaming.

"I am keeping the hybrid," Chris said, refusing to give an inch. "You said that I could, and I am holding you to your word. There is nothing for you here."

What had humanity been to Kai-Ren but a curiosity at first, and then a contagion? We'd polluted his hatchlings and caused the other Faceless to turn on him. We were as dangerous to him, in our own way, as he was to us. The question was, would he accept that or would he want revenge?

Kai-Ren would always be unknowable, even as we balanced on the knife's edge.

Kai-Ren tilted his head and looked at Cam. "Does this one speak for you, Cam-ren, my pet?"

"Yes." Cam lifted his chin. "We are home. It's over."

Kai-Ren hissed again, a displeased noise. He'd enjoyed all those little emotions that we shed like pollen when he shook us, hadn't he? He'd liked the unpredictability of them, and the way they seesawed wildly. He'd liked the taste of them. He didn't like when we were as cold as the Faceless. Where was the novelty in that?

Because all we'd ever been, however much we'd thought it was something deeper, was a novelty.

"Cam-Ren?" Then he turned his gaze to me. "Bray-dee?"

I took another step back.

Kai-Ren looked back at Cam, like a predator watching his favorite prey.

"What do you want me to say?" Cam asked, his forehead creasing. "I don't know what you want me to *say.*"

Kai-Ren narrowed his eyes.

"Listen," Cam said, and how was his voice not shaking? "Just listen, please. You hurt me. You *raped* me. And I know that you will never understand what that even means, but you took something from me that you had no right to take, and the fact that you can never understand that is exactly why I won't go with you."

Kai-Ren stared at him and said nothing.

"The treaty remains in place," Chris said. "Goodbye, Kai-Ren."

I backed away, tugging at Cam's hand. Cam stood there a moment longer, looking at Kai-Ren. Looking, and waiting for something he wanted, something he needed that would never come.

Cam had been with Kai-Ren for four years before we met, and he'd survived those four years by telling himself that Kai-Ren wasn't a nightmare, he was just *different.* An alien, not a monster. He'd survived by staring into Kai-Ren's Faceless mask and believing it was more than his own reflection staring back.

If there was a moment for Kai-Ren to prove himself something more than he was, something even remotely capable of understanding, of feeling, then this was it.

The silence stretched out under his cold yellow stare.

And then Cam let me pull him away, and we left the pod bay.

An hour later the Faceless ship detached itself from Defender Three in a blast of vented oxygen, and slid slowly back into the black.

FROM OUR ROOM IN THE OFFICERS' quarters, I watched the guys in atmo suits crawl like slow-moving ants over the Outer Ring as they repaired the breach the Faceless ship had caused. I watched the Faceless ship too, stars blinking into existence around the vanishing dark space it made as it receded into the distance.

Lucy was crashed out in the bed, blankets pulled up to her chin and her hair spread out in tangles along the pillow. She was breathing deeply, and I wondered what she was dreaming about. Did she dream of the red dirt of the gulf like I did, or hadn't she lived there long enough to have it sink into her bloodstream like it had into mine? Maybe her dreams weren't those of a reffo kid. Maybe they were different than mine. Maybe instead of looking into the past, her dreams reached for the future. I hoped they did.

Cam sat on the floor at the foot of the bed, a half-drunk can of soda on the floor beside him. I crossed the floor and sat down beside him. Stole a swig of his soda and asked, "You okay?"

Cam blinked. "I don't know. I thought..."

"You thought he'd give you something?"

Cam's mouth twitched. "Yeah. Maybe. I guess wanting him to be more... more *human* was wishful thinking. Just another way to kid myself that he wasn't entirely cold-blooded." He knocked his shoulder against mine. "I should have listened to you from the start."

"To be fair, that's pretty bad advice for most things."

He smiled faintly, and reached out and curled his fingers through mine. "I want to go home, Brady."

"Yeah?"

"I want to sleep in our bed." He squeezed my hand. "I want to wear something apart from a uniform the whole time. I want to eat the food from our refrigerator."

"That's gonna be pretty fucking revolting by now."

That won a laugh from him. "You know what I mean."

I leaned against him. "Yeah."

We were silent for a long while, listening to the faint thrum of the station and the whisper of cool air through the ducts in the ceiling. I ran the fingertips of my free hand over the dry metal floor, and luxuriated for a moment in the sensation of not being damp for the first time in months.

"I don't know what I expected," Cam said. "Maybe I just wanted some closure."

Kai-Ren was going to haunt him for a long time, probably. And I figured we could deal with that, as long as it meant he was really a ghost.

I lifted Cam's hand onto my thigh, and opened it like carefully spreading the petals of a flower. The lines on his palm were as familiar to me as the lines on my own. The life line, the heart line. There were others too, probably. Not that I believed that stuff. Just goes to show that sometimes people stared up at the stars to try and predict the future, and sometimes they stared at their own hands right in front of their faces. It was all bullshit, but I guess we were a species that believed a lot of bullshit because deep down we were all scared of the things we couldn't see coming.

I lifted Cam's hand, my fingers closing around his wrist, and kissed his palm. His skin tasted a little like salt. It was nice. I kissed his fingertips too, one by one, and he watched me with a soft expression.

"Come on," I said, and dropped his hand for a moment while I climbed to my feet. Then I reached down for him, and helped him up. I held his hand tightly as I drew him back over toward the window.

I stood behind him, and slipped my arms around his waist. His hands found mine. I rested my chin on his shoulder, and we both gazed out into the black. Into the field of stars that grew larger and larger as the Faceless ship receded into them.

Back when I'd been a recruit on Defender Three I'd hated to look into the stars. I'd hated the reminder of how small and vulnerable the station was, and how the only thing between me and asphyxiation was a thin metal wall. And knowing what was out there should have scared me even more. Should have reduced me to a gibbering mess on the floor. Facing my fears hadn't destroyed them. It had brought them into sharp relief instead, and I would probably never shed them. But I'd learned that I wasn't useless. I'd learned that I was stronger than I thought, I guess, and that even if I wasn't a hero I was a survivor. And that was something worth knowing.

I leaned into Cam and together we stood there in silence and watched the Faceless ship vanish into nothing.

CHAPTER 16

FIVE MONTHS later

I STRAIGHTENED my tunic for the hundredth time and stared down at my scuffed boots. Should probably have remembered to polish them, I guess. Still, too late now. I side-eyed the other seven crewman lined up outside the classroom, trying to pick which one of us was the obvious fucking washout. Me, probably. These guys were lugging textbooks and folders. I wasn't even sure the single pen in my pocket even worked anymore. The classroom was in a demountable building at the back of the base hospital. The other guys clustered in the narrow band of shade that ran along the side of the building. Not me. I stood in the sun, soaking up the heat. Beads of sweat formed on the nape of my neck and slid down the back of my shirt. I could feel my skin starting to burn.

At five minutes to the hour the door to the classroom was opened. I was the last one to file in. I took a seat at the front, stretched out my legs, and pulled out my pen to chew on the end. I peered at the whiteboard, and at the words scrawled there in very familiar handwriting.

Paramedic Care - Training Module 1.

The grumpy bastard in charge leaned on his desk and glared at us. "My name is Major Layton," he said. "If you're good enough, you can call me Doc."

I raised my hand.

Doc's eyebrows tugged together. "You can call me Doc, Garrett."

I grinned and lowered my hand again, and basked in the narrow glares the other students sent my way. I was gonna milk this nepotism thing as far as I could. Though it wasn't just nepotism. I had been a good medic, and both Doc and I knew it. And for guys like me, guys without university degrees, becoming a paramedic was the first step to becoming a medical officer. It meant signing on for another five years once my first ten was up, but then I could walk out with actual qualifications. And an officer's pension. It was the smart thing to do. And, unlike every other poor bastard in this classroom, I'd never have to serve on another Defender to do it. The military had agreed to keep me on the ground, and I had agreed not to fuck shit up and get thrown in the stockade anymore. It was a pretty sweet deal.

It helped, of course, that the Faceless Ambassador had made it clear that he wanted me nearby. The military still thought Thomas had the power to call Kai-Ren and the Faceless down to raze our remaining cities, and none of us were saying any different. Chris had burned quite a few notebooks before he'd turned the rest over to the war room. I wasn't sure if that made the bunch of us conspirators, or collaborators, or some other big, fancy word that would one day get thrown at us in a tribunal, but fuck it, I liked it.

Doc took a look at my empty desk, narrowed his eyes at me, and then tossed a textbook in my direction. I caught it against my chest.

"Bring your own tomorrow, Garrett," he said. "I presume you were issued with one?"

"Yeah," I said. "Thanks, Doc."

I cracked the textbook open at the table of contents, running my fingers along the crisp edges of the pages and wondering whatever happened to *General Physiology*. Sometimes those months spent on the Faceless ship felt like the strangest dream, and sometimes all it took was seeing a diagram of the chambers of the heart and I was sitting on the cot in Doc's makeshift medbay again, poring over *General Physiology* and bitching about having no cigarettes.

"Let's open up to the first chapter and get started," Doc said gruffly.

I slid down into my chair comfortably and turned the page.

EVERY FRIDAY NIGHT the guys turned up at our apartment and we ordered pizzas and drank beer. Well, Lucy and Thomas drank soda because Lucy had only just turned nine and Thomas didn't like the taste of beer. To start with Thomas had arrived every week with Chris and a pair of escorting officers, but those escorting officers soon got sick of sitting in the stairwell because they weren't invited to our party. So now Thomas turned up after dark with a hoodie pulled forward to hide his alien face, and Chris drove him. Thomas had quarters on the base, and Chris lived there with him. At first Chris had worried that Thomas would fail to thrive in our atmosphere, with our food and a hundred different viruses that he was exposed to through living surrounded by humans, but it turned out his human side was tough as nails. And so it should have been, right? It came from Kopa.

The first day he called one of the officers on the base an asshole, I knew he'd be just fine.

Doc was the first to arrive, a six-pack wedged under his arm. He'd only seen me hours before in the classroom but that didn't stop him from pulling me into a hug. Then he found room for his beer in the refrigerator, and went to see how Lucy was going with her homework.

Andre and Harry were the next to turn up. They brought the pizzas. Andre and Harry were both in intel still, and Andre was getting married in a few months to a girl who didn't think it was too weird that he'd once shared a psychic connection with a bunch of other guys and the Faceless. I mean, she thought it was weird but she was going to marry him anyway, which was probably about the best he could expect.

Chris and Thomas were the last to arrive, but the pizzas were still hot so I didn't give them too much shit for it. We sat around the living room and ate and drank and watched some bullshit movie with a bunch of car chases and explosions. I looked around the room, around at the people I cared about, and let contentment settle over me like warm water.

Life wasn't perfect. It would never be perfect. But we were still here, still living it, and that was more than a lot of people got.

Doc sat in the armchair, with Lucy sitting on the arm and chattering at him like a bird. Chris and Thomas and Andre took the couch, leaving me and Cam and Harry the floor. I didn't mind. I could reach the pizza faster from my position by the coffee table. And to think my instructor in tactical orientation back when I'd been a lowly recruit had thought I'd never learn a thing. Fuck that guy. I'll bet he wasn't eating pizza right now.

"How's class going, Brady?" Andre asked, leaning out past me to snag a piece of pizza.

I grunted and shrugged.

"He's my worst student," Doc said. "The little shit is also the smartest one in the bunch."

I grinned. "A bad attitude—"

"Is better than no attitude at all," Doc finished for me, and raised his beer in my direction.

We both knew my insolence kept him young, and that he loved me for it. He would have stayed on Defender Three if he really hated me, but he'd leapt at the chance for a teaching position planetside. And not just planetside, but at the base in Fourteen-Beta. I'd take him to Kopa one day too, I thought. To show him what it was like there. I'd take all of them. They'd seen it in my memories, but I wanted to show them it was real too. Wanted to show them how reffos had to live. Because even on nights like these when I was scarfing down pizza and beer—*especially* on nights like these—I thought a lot about how the people in townships like Kopa lived. And the more people who saw it, the more we had a chance of changing it. And maybe that was a pipe dream, and maybe I was kidding myself, but here I was in a room full of people who'd been in a battle with the Faceless and *won*. If anyone could do the impossible it was us.

"How about you, Thomas?" Andre asked. "How are things with you?"

Thomas made a so-so gesture that was new. "There is a lot to learn." He glanced at Chris. "A lot."

Chris reached for his beer, saw that it was empty, and then pushed himself off the couch to head into the kitchen for another one. Thomas followed him.

I leaned against Cam and he put an arm around me.

On the television, someone's car exploded.

I looked at the empty pizza boxes for a while, figured they wouldn't take themselves out, and stood up and carried them into the kitchen.

Chris was leaning against the counter. Thomas stood in front of him bracketing him with his arms. Chris had a hand against his chest, holding him at a slight distance. Not pushing him back, just not letting him as close as he wanted. Thomas straightened up as he heard me come in, and turned around to lean against the counter with Chris.

"There's more soda in the fridge," I told him.

Thomas smiled. "Thank you, Brady."

Thomas looked less like a Faceless these days, and it wasn't just that I was used to him now. He had a faint tan that made him less garishly white and corpse-like. He'd never be able to walk openly down a street or anything without getting stares for being weird, but those stares would mostly be from people wondering what the hell had happened to that poor guy, not thinking he was half alien.

Maybe I'd take him to Kopa too, and show him where half his DNA came from.

Thomas got his soda and headed back into the living room.

I looked at Chris.

Chris folded his arms over his chest and looked back, eyebrows raised. "What?"

I shrugged. "I was just thinking."

His posture relaxed slightly. "About what?"

"About that time you told me you were jealous of Cam because Cam had found what he was looking for."

Chris's mouth quirked.

"Thomas is stubborn," I said. "He'll wear you down eventually."

Chris snorted. "Maybe."

I chewed my lip for a moment. "He's his own person, remember? You gave him a name because of that."

"It's not that straightforward."

"Says the guy who bluffed the entire military and also told Kai-Ren to fuck off?" I waited for his wry smile of acknowledgement and then I shrugged again. "So did you? Did you get what you wanted?"

Chris smiled slightly, his gaze drifting past me to the living room. "Yeah," he said softly. "I think that maybe I did."

———

AFTER EVERYONE LEFT and Lucy was tucked up in bed, I took my pack of cigarettes from the top of the refrigerator and went and sat outside on the balcony. Cam was already there.

The night was cool and dark. Lights glinted all the way down the hill, from apartment blocks like ours. I could hear the distant whine of the train. I leaned on the balcony railing beside Cam, and took out a cigarette. Turned it over a few times, and slotted it back in the pack. Quitting was fucking hard, okay? But it turned out I was better at it if I had some cigarettes on hand, just so I remembered that not smoking them was my choice and not something forced on me by deprivation.

I tucked the pack into the pocket of my jeans and rested my

forearms on the rail again. Turned my hand palm up so that Cam could catch it in his.

Cam's face was tilted up as he drank in the night sky. He wore that expression of faint wonder he always did when he lost himself in starlight. I loved that about him, even though I'd never felt the same. There had been a time when all I'd known about the black was that all my nightmares came from there. Which was still true and always would be, but I also remembered the beauty of the clouds in the nebula, the endless spread of stars like lanterns scattered in the black, and the way the light of them caught in Cam's eyes when he smiled at me.

I held his hand tightly, filled my lungs with air, and lifted my gaze to the starlight.

AFTERWORD

Thank you so much for reading. I hope that you enjoyed it. I would very much appreciate it if you could take a few moments to leave a review on Amazon or Goodreads, or on your social media platform of choice.

ABOUT LISA HENRY

Lisa likes to tell stories, mostly with hot guys and happily ever afters.

Lisa lives in tropical North Queensland, Australia. She doesn't know why, because she hates the heat, but she suspects she's too lazy to move. She spends half her time slaving away as a government minion, and the other half plotting her escape.

She attended university at sixteen, not because she was a child prodigy or anything, but because of a mix-up between international school systems early in life. She studied History and English, neither of them very thoroughly.

Lisa has been published since 2012, and was a LAMBDA finalist for her quirky, awkward coming-of-age romance *Adulting 101*, and a Rainbow Awards finalist for 2019's *Anhaga*.

You can join Lisa's Facebook reader group at Lisa Henry's Hangout, and find her website at lisahenryonline.com.

ALSO BY LISA HENRY

Socially Orcward

Writing as Cari Waites

Stealing Innocents

Made in the USA
Las Vegas, NV
20 February 2023